Winner Takes the Cake

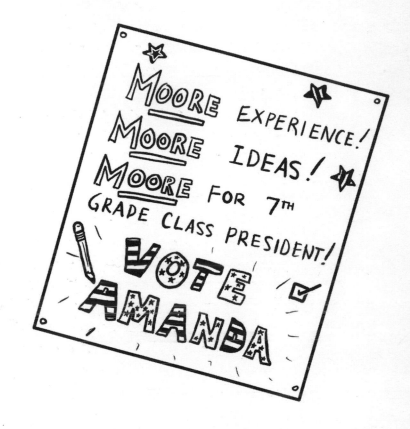

Grosset & Dunlap

For Allie Roth—D.M.

dish

#11

Winner Takes the Cake

friends, cooking, eating, talking, life.

By Diane Muldrow
Illustrated by Barbara Pollak

Grosset & Dunlap
New York

GROSSET & DUNLAP
Published by the Penguin Group
Penguin Group (USA) Inc., 375 Hudson Street, New York, New York 10014, U.S.A.
Penguin Group (Canada), 90 Eglinton Avenue East, Suite 700, Toronto, Ontario,
Canada M4P 2Y3 (a division of Pearson Penguin Canada Inc.)
Penguin Books Ltd, 80 Strand, London WC2R ORL, England
Penguin Ireland, 25 St Stephen's Green, Dublin 2, Ireland
(a division of Penguin Books Ltd)
Penguin Group (Australia), 250 Camberwell Road, Camberwell, Victoria 3124,
Australia (a division of Pearson Australia Group Pty Ltd)
Penguin Books India Pvt Ltd, 11 Community Centre, Panchsheel Park,
New Delhi - 110 017, India
Penguin Group (NZ), 67 Apollo Drive, Mairangi Bay, Auckland 1311,
New Zealand (a division of Pearson New Zealand Ltd)
Penguin Books (South Africa) (Pty) Ltd, 24 Sturdee Avenue,
Rosebank, Johannesburg 2196, South Africa

Penguin Books Ltd, Registered Offices:
80 Strand, London WC2R ORL, England

2007 Edition

Cover photo © Veer

The Library of Congress has cataloged the original edition (ISBN 0-448-43213-7) as follows:
Library of Congress Control Number: 2003016047

ISBN 978-0-448-44666-0   10 9 8 7 6 5 4 3 2 1

"**I**'m *starving!*"

Twin sisters Molly and Amanda Moore grinned at their younger brother, Matthew. "Nice to see you, too," joked Molly as she dropped her heavy backpack on the floor in the Moores' front hall. It was after six o'clock on Friday afternoon, and the twins had just gotten home from school.

"We've been waiting for you *forever,*" Matthew complained. "What took you so long?"

"Sorry, it's my fault," Amanda explained. "The school play is only a week away, and we were swamped with last-minute alterations to the costumes." Amanda, who was in the drama club at Windsor Middle School, had joined the costume crew after not being cast in the most recent school play.

"Don't take off your coats, girls," Mrs. Moore said as she walked into the hall, followed by her sister, Livia. She'd been staying with the Moores for the past week. Everyone—especially the twins—loved having fun, stylish Aunt Livia around!

"We're going out for dinner," Aunt Livia explained, hugging the twins. "Your dad will meet us there."

"Cool," said Molly. "Louie's?"

"Actually, Aunt Livia and I saw a new restaurant on Seventh Avenue—Edo Teppan-Yaki," Mom said. "It's a teppan grill."

Matthew scrunched up his face. "Teppan? I don't like teppan," he grumbled. "It tastes terrible."

"Teppan isn't a food," Mom said, smiling at Matthew. "It's a kind of Japanese cooking. Trust me, you'll love it!"

Everyone was soon bundled up in their coats and heading down the hill toward Seventh Avenue, the heart of Park Terrace, Brooklyn. Molly and Amanda loved living in Park Terrace. It seemed to have *everything*—fun and unique stores all along Seventh Avenue; beautiful Prospect Park with its skating rink, pedal boats, rolling meadows, nature trails, and band shell; and dozens of restaurants that served food as diverse as the people of Brooklyn themselves. And it was just a short subway ride under the East River to Manhattan, the heart of New York City!

"Molly, how was your Volunteers' Club meeting today?" Aunt Livia asked as she draped her arms around her two nieces.

"It was great!" exclaimed Molly. "We earned so much money at the Harvest Fair fundraiser a few weeks ago that we got this really nice thank-you letter. And guess what— it was signed by the *mayor*! Principal Wagner stopped by the meeting to congratulate us, and she said she's going to frame the letter and hang it in the front hall."

"Wonderful, sweetie!" exclaimed Mom. "You should feel so proud."

Molly nodded. "It feels awesome to help people like that." For a recent social studies assignment, Molly had researched hunger in America. She'd been shocked to learn how many people go hungry in America every single day—and had vowed to find a way to help however she could.

"Here we are," Aunt Livia said suddenly, stopping in front of a small restaurant with large glass windows. The twins could see their father waiting in the entryway inside, rumpling his hair while studying a menu.

"Hey, everybody," Dad said with a smile as they entered the restaurant. "This place looks—"

"Wow! This is *awesome*!" Matthew interrupted him. A teakwood bridge arched over a small indoor pond filled with smooth stones and *koi*—large, brightly-colored Japanese fish. A gentle waterfall provided a calm, soothing atmosphere. Single-file, the Moores crossed the bridge into the main part of the restaurant, which was decorated with paper screens and richly-colored Japanese prints. But the best part of the restaurant was the seating area. Instead of tables and chairs arranged throughout the main room, Edo Teppan-Yaki had five gleaming silver surfaces that were edged on three sides with polished wooden countertops. Eight tall chairs were pulled up to three sides of the tables.

A smiling woman in a glistening green-and-gold kimono approached them, bowing slightly. "Welcome to Edo Teppan-Yaki," she said softly. "We are so pleased to serve you tonight. Six?"

"Yes," Aunt Livia confirmed. The Moores followed the hostess to one of the odd-looking tables.

"Have you eaten teppan before?" asked the hostess. The adults nodded, but the kids just looked puzzled.

"No," Molly answered. "But we love Japanese food."

"Wonderful," smiled the hostess. "In teppan cooking, all of the food is prepared right at the table by a master chef. You are served the freshest, most inspired dishes and are able to watch your chef prepare them. I am certain you will find teppan a fascinating cooking style—and very delicious!"

After the Moores sat at the table, the hostess gave them menus and then returned to the front of the restaurant. Now that the twins were closer to the tables, they could tell that the gleaming surfaces were actually grills surrounded by bottles of oils, vinegars, and spices. Molly turned to Amanda. "I can't believe a real chef is going to cook right here!" she exclaimed.

"I know," Amanda said, nodding her head. "Too cool!" She opened her menu. One side had dishes listed in English under the headings, "Sushi," "Traditional," "Side Orders," and "Special." The other side of the menu was covered with Japanese writing.

"Hey, Matthew," Molly teased. "How about some sushi? *Mmm*, raw fish!"

"No way," he replied, shaking his head vehemently. "I want that really good fried shrimp stuff. With sticky rice."

"You mean shrimp tempura, sport," Dad told Matthew.

"Yakisoba is excellent," recommended Aunt Livia as she glanced at her menu. "It's a wonderful dish of fried curly noodles, like ramen, with vegetables, pork, and a thick sauce. And I *love* sushi, Matthew! I'm getting some for an appetizer and you have to try it."

"Okay," Matthew agreed. "If you say it's so great." But he didn't sound too sure.

"Molls, do you want to split some sushi for an appetizer?" Amanda asked.

"Sure," replied Molly.

"What looks good for an entrée?" Dad asked the twins.

"Chicken teriyaki," they replied at the same time. Everyone laughed.

"The twin thing again!" Aunt Livia smiled. That's what the twins called it whenever they said or thought the same thing at the same time—which happened a lot.

Although Molly and Amanda were identical twins with long brown hair, freckles, and bright green eyes, it was easy to tell them apart. Molly preferred high ponytails and low-top sneakers to fancy hairstyles and funky shoes, and would rather play sports than go shopping. Amanda was the fashion-conscious one, always experimenting with new looks. Tonight was no exception. While Molly sported her favorite jeans and a red sweatshirt with "Brooklyn" on the front, Amanda was decked out in a green top with a silver paisley pattern over flared brown cords and cute brown ankle boots.

Just then, a man wearing white chef's clothes approached their table. Across his forehead was a white band with a red rising sun design. He bowed, grinning broadly. "Welcome to Edo Teppan-Yaki!" he exclaimed. "My name is Chef Kaga and I hope you're all hungry!" He picked up a gleaming flat spatula and twirled it, tossing it high in the air and catching it gracefully. Chef Kaga turned to Matthew and pointed the spatula at him. "You must be the one in charge. Sir, I am delighted to serve you this evening." Then Chef Kaga bowed to Matthew, making the boy giggle.

Chef Kaga turned to Molly and Amanda, flipping the spatula behind his back before pointing it at them. "Twins! Twice as nice! Ladies, your wish is my command." Finally, he faced Mom, Dad, and Aunt Livia. "Boy and girls, would you like to order from the kiddie menu tonight?" That was too much for Matthew, who started laughing.

Chef Kaga straightened up and snapped his fingers loudly. As if by magic, two assistants appeared pushing a three-tiered cart laden with fresh vegetables, raw meat, and fish. "Here is your dinner," Chef Kaga announced. "My work here is done."

The twins looked at all the raw food and shook their heads, puzzled. Then Chef Kaga slapped his head. "*Whoops!* I forgot to cook it!" Laughing at his own corny joke, Chef Kaga asked, "What would you like to eat tonight?"

Molly noticed that as everyone ordered, Chef Kaga nodded, but wrote nothing down. She leaned over to Amanda and whispered, "This guy's *good!*"

"Excellent choices," Chef Kaga said, beaming. "Teppan-yaki is a relatively new style of Japanese cooking—only two hundred years old. But in Japan, freshness and presentation have always been very important parts of food preparation. Teppan-yaki adds the excitement of a performing chef who cooks right at your table!"

While Chef Kaga spoke, he began expertly slicing vegetables. The knife moved so quickly in his skilled hands that it was just a flash of silver. After Chef Kaga had sliced cabbage, mushrooms, carrots, broccoli, sweet potatoes, and scallions, he pushed each vegetable into a separate pile. He did the same with chicken, beef, and fish. With one hand, he poured golden cooking oil onto the grill in front of him, then spread it around to each corner with the flat spatula.

The twins watched in amazement as Chef Kaga cooked all six meals on the grill in front of them—at the same time! With the flat spatula in one hand and the long chopstick in the other, Chef Kaga sautéed the chicken and beef, stir-fried the vegetables, cooked the scrambled eggs, fried the rice, and grilled the fish.

"How does he *do* that?" wondered Amanda.

"Years of practice!" replied Chef Kaga.

In about ten minutes, each meal was ready. Chef Kaga artfully arranged the food on beautiful china plates with Japanese designs on them. From a sushi bar on the side of the restaurant, Chef Kaga's assistant brought several small plates of sushi to the table.

Chef Kaga bowed low as the Moores thanked him. "My pleasure! I hope to see you all back soon!" He moved to another table that had filled up with hungry patrons, eager to watch Chef Kaga's cooking performance and eat the delicious food.

The fragrant dishes, which had been cooked just moments before, smelled wonderful to the twins. "*Mmm*! This is delicious!" Molly exclaimed after her first bite of chicken. "I love the marinade—it's salty and tangy."

"Ish aweshum," Matthew mumbled with his mouth full. Bits of rice sprayed onto the table.

"Gross!" squealed Amanda.

Dad raised his eyebrows. "Mind your manners, sport."

With his mouth tightly closed, Matthew nodded.

"Barb, try some of my yakisoba," Aunt Livia encouraged. "Let's share like the twins."

"Great idea," Mom replied. "This is my favorite part of eating out—getting to try new things! And it's even better when the food is so fresh and delicious. It's so nice to take a break from cooking, isn't it, girls?

"*Definitely*," Amanda replied emphatically. "But I'll be back in the kitchen tomorrow. Dish has a four-dinner job for the Myers."

Dish was a cooking business that Molly and Amanda had started over a year ago. It all started one boring summer day when Molly, who was sick of the takeout their busy parents kept bringing home, had the great idea to surprise their parents and cook dinner for the whole family. Amanda wasn't sure they could do it, but together the twins had found a recipe, gone to the grocery store, and made chicken picatta, wild rice, and salad. And it was *delicious*!

The twins had had such a blast cooking that dinner that they'd decided to take a cooking class for kids at Park Terrace Cookware with their best friend, Shawn Jordan. At class, they'd run into Peichi Cheng and Natasha Ross, who they knew from school. It wasn't long before the five girls had formed a cooking club. Soon, the cooking club turned into a cooking business when the girls realized that the Moores weren't the only family in Park Terrace who were too busy to cook dinner every night. By offering fresh, home-cooked meals to busy families, Dish became an instant success! Since those first summer days of Dish, the Chef Girls (as they called themselves) had had some amazing experiences, including cooking for fancy parties, appearing on live TV, and, most recently, helping those in need.

It wasn't always easy for the Chef Girls to balance homework, after-school activities, and their business. Recently, for Molly, it had all become too much. Already busy with baby-sitting, writing for the school newspaper, and fundraising for the Windsor Volunteers' Club, Molly had been so upset to find out how many families in America are hungry that she had decided to start a new business. By bottling and selling her delicious pesto sauce, Molly would be able to donate all of the profits to local food banks. But working on two businesses was overwhelming, and Molly had made the difficult decision to leave Dish. It had shocked the girls—especially Amanda—but they tried to be understanding. Still, Dish just wasn't the same without Molly.

Even though leaving Dish had been Molly's decision, she felt uncomfortable talking about it. She cleared her throat. "Tomorrow, I'm covering the Windsor football game against the Bergen Bears," she told her parents. "I want to cover more sports for *the Post*. I really love writing articles."

"Just like your Aunt Livia!" Mom said with a smile.

Aunt Livia, a freelance writer, wrote all kinds of articles for magazines and newspapers. Mom turned to Dad and changed the subject. "By the way, Professor Stephens, the head of the art history department, presented me with an interesting offer today." Mom was a professor of art history at Brooklyn College.

"Oh? What's that?" asked Dad, reaching for some of Molly's sushi with his chopsticks.

"He was supposed to attend the annual 'Art through the Ages' conference at King's College in London," Mom began. "But he won't be able to make it. He asked if I'd take his place. But I just don't see how it could work out. The conference is two weeks long—and I'd have to leave next Tuesday."

"What?" cried Aunt Livia. "You're kidding, right, Barbara? This is a fantastic opportunity! You've *got* to go to London."

The twins smiled at each other. They were doing the "twin thing" again, thinking how much Aunt Livia sounded like Mom just then.

"I agree," Dad said, smiling at Mom. "An all-expenses-paid trip to London? How could you refuse? And it will be great for your career, too. I can hold down the fort around here."

Aunt Livia looked at Dad. "Mike, you should go with her! A romantic trip to London for just the two of you? It will be like a second honeymoon! I can stay on and take care of the kids."

"It *would* be a wonderful experience," Mom began. "But Livvy, you're supposed to leave for California on Sunday."

Aunt Livia shrugged and waved her hand in the air. "Please—I'd much rather spend another few weeks with my favorite nieces and nephew," she said with a grin. "I can call my editor on Monday and work from here for the next few weeks." She looked at Molly. "One of the great things about being a freelance writer is flexibility. It sounds like a career *you* would like!"

"Well," Mom said, "I'd love to go to London. What do you say, Mike?"

"Absolutely! When do we leave?" Dad replied. "I still have some vacation time at work, so that shouldn't be a problem."

"*Oooh*, can I go, too?" exclaimed Amanda. "I would love to see the theater district, and the new Globe Theater!" She grinned. "Oh, please, Mum!" she said in her best British accent. "I would so *veddy* much like to go to London!"

"Yeah, let us go, too, Mom," Molly echoed. "Maybe hanging out with real British people would help Amanda do a better British accent!" she teased her sister. Amanda made a face at Molly and poked her in the arm.

"Not this time, girls," Mom said kindly. "I'd love to take all three of you with us, but you need to be in school. We'll go together another time."

"Oh, all right," Amanda sighed.

"Manda, it will be way more fun here," Molly said with a grin. "Just us kids and Aunt Livia! Woo-hoo! Par-tay!"

Everyone at the table started to laugh—except for Matthew, who'd gotten very quiet since Mom said the word "London."

"**H**i, Shawn!" Molly said with a smile as she opened the Moores' front door the next morning. Shawn was the first to arrive for the Dish cooking job. Amanda had overslept and was now scurrying around the twins' large room upstairs, trying to get ready. Mom, Dad, Matthew, and Aunt Livia had just left for a New York Giants football game.

"Hi, Molly," Shawn replied. Shawn looked great, as always. Her brick-red sweater set off her cocoa-colored skin perfectly, and her jeans had small red roses embroidered along the pockets and hems. Shawn's red cat's-eye glasses brought the outfit together. "Are you going out?" she asked, noticing that Molly was wearing her boys' high-top canvas sneakers.

Molly nodded. "Yeah. I'm covering the Warriors football game for *the Post* today." She cleared her throat. Suddenly, Molly felt guilty about leaving while the rest of her friends spent the day cooking for Dish. Fortunately, the doorbell rang again.

Saved by the bell, thought Molly.

"*Hiiiiiiiiiiii-eeeee!*" squealed Peichi. "*Brrr!* It's starting to get *cold* out! You can really tell winter's on the way!

Molly, I'm gonna hang up my coat, okay? Amanda! Where are you?"

Molly and Shawn grinned at each other. Peichi was always so lively and talkative! It was hard to feel awkward when she was around.

Amanda came rushing downstairs just then. "Hey! I can't believe I slept until—"

Ding-dong!

"That must be Natasha," Molly said, opening the door again. Sure enough,

Natasha Ross stood on the doorstep. She looked cute in her pale purple wool coat and was wearing a new purple and blue beret over her chin-length blonde hair.

"*Oooh!* I so love your beret!" exclaimed Amanda. "It's adorable."

Natasha smiled shyly. "Thanks! Laure sent it to me. Isn't she the best?" Natasha had met her friend Laure during her summer trip to Paris with her mother. The two girls had become good friends, and stayed in touch after Natasha had returned to Brooklyn.

"Okay! Everybody's here. Let's get cookin'!" Amanda announced, turning toward the kitchen. The Chef Girls followed her down the hall. They loved spending time in the Moores' spacious, bright kitchen, which was painted a pale, buttery yellow with accents of blue and green tiles that Mom had bought in Spain. There was a large island in the middle of the room that was perfect for food prep.

Large cupboards with glass doors showed off Mom and Dad's collection of funky dishes, and scrolled hooks attached to the ceiling held gleaming copper pots and pans.

Amanda unfolded a piece of paper on the island and glanced it over. "The Myers cooking job: chicken and dumplings, pork chops with mushroom sauce, shepherd's pie, and—of course—lasagna. For vegetables, we'll make broccoli with garlic sauce, and peas and carrots. And salad. Apple cookies and brownies for dessert. *Hmmm*—maybe we can make some rolls, too, if we have time."

"Wow, that's a lot of new recipes," Molly commented from the doorway.

Amanda smiled at her twin. "I thought it might be nice to mix things up a bit. We were making so many old standbys, you know?" She turned to Shawn, Natasha, and Peichi. "Since there are four of us, we can each cook a main dish. Then we'll split up the vegetables and desserts. Okay?"

The friends nodded in agreement and began to get out the ingredients they'd need. Suddenly, Molly felt self-conscious standing in the doorway. For some reason, she didn't want to enter the kitchen. It just seemed so, well, *weird* to not be cooking with Dish, to not be right in the middle of everything. *Amanda's totally taken over,* Molly realized. *It's like they don't need me at all. It's like—like I don't belong in my own kitchen.*

"Well, I'm leaving for the game," Molly said abruptly.

"Have a good day, guys! Uh, maybe I'll see you when I get back later."

The game didn't start for another hour, but—even though leaving Dish was her decision—Molly needed to escape this terrible feeling she had—of not belonging anymore.

A few hours later, the Chef Girls took a lunch break. The kitchen was filled with delicious smells—chicken, vegetables, and dumplings simmering in broth; mushrooms and onions slowly cooking to form a thick sauce for the pork chops; fudgey brownies baking in the oven.

Peichi inhaled deeply. "It smells *great* in here!" she exclaimed. "I can't believe we're cooking such great food, but we're sitting around eating boring sandwiches! No fair!"

The Chef Girls cracked up.

"That gives me an idea," Natasha spoke up. "We should cook more dinners for ourselves. Like, once a month or something. We used to do that, but Dish got so busy we put *ourselves* on the back burner."

"That sounds good," Amanda commented as she popped a baby carrot in her mouth. She glanced at the clock hanging above the sink. "I can't believe it's after two o'clock already! We still have to make the cookies and the vegetable dishes."

"It *is* taking a little longer today," Shawn agreed. "Without Molly."

The girls looked at one another. Shawn had just said what they'd all been thinking.

"It's, uh, weird," Natasha began. "I know we were doing a lot of jobs without Molly before she, uh, officially left Dish. But it still feels...different now that it's, you know, more real."

"You guys? Do you think maybe we should find a new member?" said Peichi.

Amanda nodded slowly. "I just...I keep hoping Molly will just change her mind and come back to Dish. But it couldn't hurt to have a few alternate members. Let's make a list of people we could ask to fill in." She tore a piece of paper off the magnetic notepad attached to the fridge.

"How about Connor, Omar, and Justin?" Natasha suggested. "They've helped out Dish before."

"No *way*," Peichi said firmly, shaking her head. The girls giggled. Omar Kazdan had a huge crush on Peichi and was always looking for excuses to hang out with her. Peichi liked Omar as a friend—but that was *it*!

"I agree," Amanda said quickly. "It would be, uh, weird to just have one boy helping at a time, and the rest of Dish be girls."

For months, Amanda had had a crush on cute Justin McElroy, and was always excited about having him around. Something had changed, though—and Shawn was

18

the only one of the Chef Girls who knew about it. Over the summer, Justin had developed a crush on Molly. It had hurt Amanda when she found out. But a few weeks earlier, Amanda had realized that she and Justin didn't actually have much to say to each other. She was over him now—but she still didn't feel like hanging out with him a lot.

"Okay," Shawn said sensitively, guessing why Amanda had vetoed the boys. "What about Elizabeth?"

Natasha shrugged. "We've invited her to do Dish before. I just don't think cooking is really her thing." Elizabeth Derring was in seventh grade with the Chef Girls at Windsor Middle School. She and her aunt Paula had moved to Brooklyn from Minnesota last spring. They rented the top floor of Natasha's house.

"Well, it's not like we have to figure it out right now," Amanda said practically. "It's just something we can keep in mind."

BRRIIINNNGGG!

Everyone jumped as the timer rang.

"Break's over!" giggled Peichi, getting up to take the brownies out of the oven. "Back to work!"

That night after dinner, Molly wandered into the kitchen, where Aunt Livia was flipping through a magazine and drinking a cup of berry tea.

"Hello, darling," Aunt Livia said when she saw Molly, her face crinkling into the large, warm smile that always made Molly feel like she was the most special person in the world. Aunt Livia held out her arm, and Molly leaned in for a quick hug.

"I'm glad you're not going home tomorrow," Molly said, breathing in the warm, sweet fragrance of lavender, the scent of Aunt Livia's favorite soap.

"Me, too, love," Aunt Livia said. She pulled out a chair at the kitchen table. "Sit and tell me about your day. You seem a little down."

Molly shrugged as she sat. "Yeah. I don't know. I had a good day, going to the game and working on my article. But it was really weird when everybody came over for Dish. I felt like I didn't belong anymore. And Dish was always, like, my thing."

Aunt Livia nodded, as if she knew exactly what Molly meant. "Do you regret leaving Dish now?" she asked gently.

Molly shook her head. "Not really. I still want to do my pesto business. But it won't be as much fun as Dish, doing it by myself."

"Maybe I can help you get the new business off the ground," Aunt Livia said thoughtfully.

"Oh, would you?" Molly asked eagerly. "I think it would feel less...overwhelming if there was somebody I could talk to about it!"

"I'd love to, Molly!" Aunt Livia replied. "Let's get started this week!"

Molly leaned over and gave Aunt Livia a quick kiss. Suddenly, everything about starting up her own pesto business seemed more manageable—and a lot more fun.

In homeroom on Monday morning, Amanda tried to stifle a yawn as she eased herself into her uncomfortable wooden chair. Next to her, Molly started to yawn, too. "No more staying up late with Aunt Livia on school nights," Amanda whispered to her twin. Mom had *not* been happy the night before when she passed by the twins' room and found the light still on, the twins and Aunt Livia whispering and giggling.

As the bell signaling the start of homeroom rang, tall, blonde Angie Martinez rushed in through the door, laughing loudly and snapping her gum. "Miss Martinez. Gum in the garbage, please," said Ms. Lopez, raising her eyebrows. Rolling her eyes so that only the students could see, Angie flounced over to the trash can to spit out her gum.

Amanda turned around in her seat and shot Molly a look. They were doing the "twin thing" again, thinking, *Angie is so annoying!* As Amanda faced forward, she saw Angie turning to stare at her from the front row, her eyes narrowed. Angie's ugly expression made Amanda uncomfortable, but she looked straight ahead as if she hadn't noticed Angie at all.

This wasn't the first time that Angie had bothered Amanda. And Amanda wasn't Angie's only target, either. The Chef Girls had met Angie at the start of sixth grade, when Angie and Shawn, who were both on the cheerleading squad, had become close friends. It had been especially painful for Molly and Amanda to watch Shawn, their oldest and best friend, drift away...but there was nothing they could do to stop it. Soon, Shawn was eating lunch with Angie almost every day, despite the nasty way Angie treated Shawn's other friends.

However, everything had changed when Angie crossed the line. Before a huge cheerleading competition last June, Angie had destroyed Elizabeth Derring's shoes out of jealousy. Elizabeth had been the team star, and Angie's actions had kept her out of the meet. Angie had been so caught up in her evil act that she hadn't noticed Shawn coming into the locker room. Shawn had seen the whole thing—and had been faced with the difficult decision of whether or not to turn Angie in. In the end, Shawn had told Coach Carson about Angie's actions. For Shawn, the friendship was over.

But being caught hadn't stopped Angie from being awful. She was just more careful now.

A voice crackled over the PA system and the room was filled with the sound of chairs scraping against the floor as the students stood for the Pledge of Allegiance. After, the student council president read a list of announcements. Amanda doodled in her notebook as she listened.

"...Windsor Middle School's Drama Club will present the play *An American Journey* this Thursday, Friday, and Saturday nights at seven o'clock in the auditorium...try-outs for the Windsor gymnastics team will be held today at three o'clock in the gym...elections for class officers will be held in three weeks. Any student wishing to run for class office should attend the informational meeting Wednesday after school..."

I can't believe the play is this weekend, Amanda thought. *That means auditions for the next play will be pretty soon—maybe next month. I hope I get a part in that one! I can't wait to be onstage again.*

A bell announced the end of homeroom, and Amanda shook herself out of her thoughts. "See you, Molls," she called to her sister, who was heading off to math class. For the second year in a row, the twins still didn't have any classes together!

Amanda squeezed into the crowded hallway that was full of students hurrying off to first period. Mr. Degregorio's classroom was just down the hall from her homeroom, so Amanda was usually one of the first students to arrive.

"Miss Moore, welcome," Mr. Degregorio said with a funny smile as she entered. "My favorite early bird!" Amanda grinned. Mr. D., as the students called him, was one of the best-loved teachers at Windsor Middle School. When Mr. D. taught, even the dull parts of social studies became fascinating. His classes were always engaging, full of interesting facts and corny jokes.

"Hi, Mr. D.," Amanda answered as she dropped her books on her desk. The only thing Amanda *didn't* like about Mr. D.'s class was that she sat right next to Angie. Even though Amanda and Angie were in the same homeroom, Angie usually didn't get to Mr. D.'s class until just before the bell rang.

BRRRIIINNNGGG!

"All right, people, let's settle down," Mr. Degregorio said. Instantly, the class quieted down to listen to him. "I'm sure you all heard the announcement a few minutes ago about class officer elections. As faculty advisor to the student council, I want to encourage each one of you to consider running for office. Being a part of student council is an opportunity to make a difference here at Windsor Middle School. Kids, I know this place isn't perfect. But we can't make it better without your ideas and opinions! Each meeting is an open forum for class officers to be the voice of their fellow students. This is your chance to be heard. Democracy in action—it's a beautiful thing, people. A beautiful thing. And, you know, in six short years you'll all be old enough to vote in state and national elections. You'll be able to vote for the mayor, the governor, the president! Which brings me to today's topic: the electoral college."

As Mr. Degregorio began class, Amanda pictured herself as seventh-grade class president—talking with students, meeting with teachers, debating issues that affected everyone at Windsor Middle School. *This sounds so cool,* she thought. *I could really enjoy this.*

After school that day, Molly got to go straight home. For once, she didn't have a meeting for the school newspaper or the Windsor Volunteers' Club. She smiled as she walked into the Moores' dignified brick townhouse, remembering how nice it felt to have the entire afternoon and evening ahead of her.

"Hello, sweetness!" Aunt Livia stood in the doorway of the Moores' cheery kitchen. She was wearing a blue-and-yellow plaid apron smeared with flour. "How was school today?"

Molly inhaled deeply. "It was good. Hey, something smells *awesome!* What are you cooking?" she asked.

"One of my all-time favorites—beef Stroganoff," Aunt Livia answered. "I thought I'd surprise your parents by having dinner ready when they get home tonight. They'll be so busy packing that cooking dinner is the last thing they need to worry about! It's practically done—we just reheat it, stir in some sour cream to make a rich sauce, and it'll be ready to eat!"

"Yum!" Molly cheered. "I can't wait." She grabbed a bright red apple from the wire basket in which Mom kept fresh fruit.

"Aren't those apples delish?" Aunt Livia asked. "I went to the farmers' market by Prospect Park this morning and got a whole basket."

"Man, you have the best days," joked Molly. "Hanging out, going to the farmers' market, cooking! I want your life!"

Aunt Livia tapped Molly playfully with a wooden spoon. "I *did* work today, young lady," she replied. "I drafted an outline for an article about scuba diving for *Seafarer Magazine.* Anyway, where's Amanda? Matthew came through like a whirlwind and grabbed a few cookies before zooming over to Ben's house. I'm sure we won't see him until dinnertime."

"Amanda's at the first dress rehearsal for the play," Molly reported. "She has to make sure the costumes don't need any more work. Hey, do you mind talking about my pesto business for a little while?"

"I'd be happy to," Aunt Livia replied.

"Thanks! Be right back," said Molly. She raced upstairs to the twins' large room and grabbed a green notebook on which she'd written *Molly's Amazing Pesto Business!!!* Returning to the kitchen, Molly opened the notebook to a page covered with numbers. "See, I originally thought that I'd buy all the ingredients," Molly told Aunt Livia. "But Peichi's mom grows basil in her garden during the spring and summer. So I thought, hey, if I grow my own basil, that'll save money, and I'll make higher profits. What do you think?"

Aunt Livia put on her reading glasses, the ones with the cool tortoise frames she'd gotten in Italy. She glanced over Molly's notes. "I think that's a super idea, Molls," she said. "I'm so proud of you! These numbers look pretty good."

"I found a place online where I can buy glass jars wholesale for bottling the pesto," Molly said proudly. "That will save me seventy-five cents a jar!"

Aunt Livia grinned. "What a savvy businesswoman!" she said proudly. Then she glanced at the clock. "We have time to go to the gardening store on Seventh Avenue. You could start growing the basil this week!"

"Awesome!" replied Molly. She jumped up from the kitchen table. "I'll get our coats!"

A few minutes later, Molly and Aunt Livia were walking down tree-lined Taft Street toward Seventh Avenue. Autumn in New York had been mild so far, and the trees still had most of their yellow and brown leaves. Molly knew that in a few weeks, Dad would have his annual Yard Work Sunday, and all of the Moores would spend the entire day in the yard, raking leaves, planting bulbs, and straightening the garden. Well, *most* of the

Moores would be working—Matthew was usually too busy jumping into piles of leaves to get much done!

Before long, Molly and Aunt Livia arrived at Seeds & Such, a cool gardening store on Seventh Avenue where Mom always bought bulbs, seeds, and gardening supplies. A tiny bell chimed as Molly and Aunt Livia entered the store. Everywhere Molly looked there were miniature bonsai trees, potted orchids, shiny green ivy, and flowers in every color of the rainbow.

"Good afternoon, ladies. Anything I can help you with?" asked a short, older man who was wearing a white apron smudged with dirt. He was standing behind a long table covered with small terra-cotta pots, bright red and orange chrysanthemums, and potting soil.

"Hi, um, yes, I want to grow some basil," Molly said.

The man nodded. "Sure, of course. Most people around here start their herb gardens in the springtime, but you shouldn't have too much trouble if you keep it indoors in a warm, sunny place—preferably on a windowsill."

Molly nodded. "I could do that, I guess."

"Now, which kind of basil would you like?" asked the shopkeeper. "I've got lemon basil, Greek basil...I'm all out of opal basil seeds, but I could order some."

"Um, just regular basil, I guess," Molly said hesitantly.

Aunt Livia spoke up. "What's the best basil for pesto sauce?" she asked.

"Ah, yes—sweet basil. And I've got some great potting soil here—it's full of nutrients that will help your plants grow strong."

"And let's get some of those cheery mums for your mom," Aunt Livia suggested to Molly. "They'll look great on the front steps!"

After the shopkeeper rang up Molly's basil seeds, soil, and pots, she proudly paid him with money she'd earned from Dish. *That pretty much wipes out my savings,* Molly thought as she pocketed a few dollars. *I hope the Brewsters call me to baby-sit again soon!*

A few minutes later, Molly and Aunt Livia headed down Seventh Avenue toward home, their arms laden with pots, soil, seed packets, and the chrysanthemums. *Here we go!* thought Molly. *It's gonna happen! My pesto business is gonna be a real thing!*

An hour later, all of the Moores were home—and hungry. Amanda tossed a fresh green salad with ranch dressing, Molly set the table, and Aunt Livia stirred sour cream into the bubbling beef Stroganoff.

"Back off, buddy," Amanda teased her brother, lifting the salad out of his reach as he tried to steal a crouton. "Did you wash your hands?"

"Um, I washed them at school today," Matthew

protested. "They're still clean!"

"Not clean enough—go scrub."

Matthew pouted as he made his way to the sink.

"Thanks so much for making dinner, Livvy," Mom said gratefully. "Mike and I have barely started to pack—this is a huge help."

"You'll have such a great time in London!" said Aunt Livia. "Take lots of pictures to show us when you get home."

Soon, everyone was seated at the table eating the rich, flavorful dinner.

"Hey, Manda, how was the first dress rehearsal today?" Molly asked.

Amanda looked up from her plate. "Huh? Oh, it was good. I feel...I dunno...less excited than I usually do during performance week. Probably because I'm not onstage, so I don't feel nervous. But it's still fun and all." She cleared her throat. "But guess what? I want to run for seventh-grade class president!"

"That's fantastic, Amanda!" Dad exclaimed, putting down his fork. "When did you decide to do this?"

Yeah, wondered Molly, surprised that Amanda hadn't mentioned it to her.

"Just today," Amanda replied. "There was this announcement about it in homeroom? And then Mr. Degregorio—he's the faculty advisor—talked about student council in social studies class. It sounds so great—'cause

31

you get to help make Windsor Middle School a better place. And there's fun stuff, too, like planning school trips and events."

"You'd be a great president, Manda," Aunt Livia said as she took a second helping of salad.

"Yeah," cracked Matthew. "President of the Fashion Society."

"Don't tease your sister, Matthew," Mom said. "She would—*will* be a great president! What's your platform going to be?"

Amanda looked at her mother blankly. "My platform?" All she could think of was platform shoes. *What's Mom talking about?*

"Yes, your platform. It's what candidates run on—their ideas and the things they want to change," Mom explained.

Amanda raised her eyebrows. "Oh, um, I haven't really figured that out yet," she admitted.

"Don't worry," Molly said to her twin. "You'll think of something. Hey, I'd love to help out with your campaign! And I bet the rest of the Chef Girls will, too. President Moore—I like the sound of that!"

"Thanks, Molls," Amanda smiled. "But will you have time? I know how crazy-busy you've been with *the Post* and the Volunteers' Club and everything. And now you're starting your own business..."

"Don't worry, Manda, I'll make time," Molly assured

her sister.

"That's what sisters do," Mom said, winking at Aunt Livia across the table. "Right, Livvy?"

Aunt Livia winked back, giggling. "Right, Babs!"

Molly and Amanda smiled at each other. It was always fun to watch Mom and Aunt Livia act like teenagers whenever they were together!

4

 amanda couldn't wait to tell her friends about running for seventh-grade class president. Finally, at lunchtime, they were all together in the cafeteria. But before she had a chance to make her big announcement, Peichi poked at her lunch. "*Eww*," she complained. "Gross-out baked beans and rubbery hot dogs. Last night, my mom and I made this awesome stir-fry with chicken, peppers, water chestnuts, and  this really delicious ginger sauce. It was *sooo* good! So I packed up a container of leftovers to bring for lunch today. But when I got up this morning, it was *gone*! My mom looked all guilty and told me that in the middle of the night, she woke up and was, like, *starving*, so she ate the whole thing! *And* she ate half a bag of cookies! I couldn't believe it! That's, like, totally *not* my mom!" Peichi paused to take a deep breath. After twelve years as an only child, Peichi had recently gotten a big surprise— her mother was expecting a baby!

"Our mom was the same way when she was pregnant with Matthew," Molly told Peichi. "She ate *all* the time— a whole head of broccoli every day. And she ate weird stuff, too—like watermelon with peanut butter on it. I mean, I like peanut butter on apples, but *watermelon?*"

"She got really big, too," Amanda added. "Right before Matthew was born, she was so big she couldn't pick up something if she dropped it on the floor! Molly and I were always running around helping her out. Remember, Molls?"

Molly smiled at her twin, thinking about how much fun they'd had when they were little kids and their brother was just a tiny baby. They were just old enough to look out for him and take care of him—but still have fun with him when they visited their grandfather Poppy at the New Jersey shore and went on family trips.

"My mom is bigger already," Peichi said. "She bought a bunch of new clothes last weekend and I helped her pick them out. It's fun and all, getting ready for the baby. But now I'm gonna remember to always cook extra! 'Cause school lunch is *nasty* today."

"So what else is new?" Shawn joked.

"That's it!" Amanda exclaimed suddenly. "That's my platform!"

The Chef Girls looked at her in confusion. "Your what?" Natasha asked.

But Molly knew exactly what her twin was talking about. "Hey, that's perfect!"

"What are you guys talking about?" Shawn asked, looking puzzled.

Amanda turned to her friends. "Guess what?

I've decided to run for seventh-grade class president!"

The Chef Girls looked at her and shrieked.

Amanda went on, "When Peichi was complaining about the school lunches, I realized that that's something I could work to change."

"Go, Manda!" Shawn said. "You could plan all kinds of new menus."

"Yeah—stuff the kids would really want to eat!" added Natasha enthusiastically.

"You've got my vote!" Peichi smiled at Amanda.

"Thanks, guys. You're awesome," Amanda said to her friends. She cleared her throat. "Um, I was wondering—do any of you want to work on my campaign? Molly's going to be my campaign manager and I was hoping you guys could help out, too. If you have time, I mean."

"Totally," exclaimed Shawn. "You'd be a really cool class prez." Peichi and Natasha nodded enthusiastically.

"Thanks, guys! You're the best!" Amanda grinned at her friends.

The bell rang, and the girls started packing up their trash.

"There's an informational meeting after school tomorrow, so I'll find out everything then. See you later!" Amanda said to the Chef Girls as they hurried off to fifth period.

After school, Shawn headed to the gym for cheer-leading practice. She stopped in the doorway as she saw Angie talking loudly with three or four other cheerleaders in the gym. After Angie had destroyed Elizabeth's shoes, she'd been suspended from cheerleading for the summer and fall—but the suspension was almost over. Next Monday, Angie would be back on the squad. Shawn wasn't sure what to expect—when she had ended their friendship, Angie had not handled it well. Whenever Shawn and Angie were in the same room, Angie seemed to be talking behind Shawn's back, excluding her, or staring at her with a look of hatred.

Just then, Angie turned around and saw Shawn entering the gym. Her brown eyes narrowed as she glared at Shawn. Then she whipped her long hair around as she bent down to whisper to Jenn, Ashley, and Rachel.

This is so stupid, Shawn thought, feeling her face grow hot. *Angie and I have got to be able to be in the same room together.*

Shawn squared her shoulders and walked over to Angie and the other girls.

"Hey, guys," Shawn said casually, trying to keep her voice steady. "What's up?"

"Not much," Rachel responded. Jenn and Ashley smiled weakly. "Angie was just telling us about—"

"Actually, it's private," Angie snapped. She smiled coldly at Shawn. "Do you mind, Shawn? I just need to talk to my *friends* for a few more minutes before

37

practice starts. Why don't you...go change or something?"

Shawn stared at Angie, then glanced at the other cheerleaders. They looked uncomfortable and refused to meet Shawn's eyes.

"Fine," Shawn replied. "I'm really not interested, anyway." She turned on her heel and walked off to the locker room.

 As Shawn spun the dial on her combination lock, she realized how miserable Angie could make cheerleading if she wanted to. Suddenly, Shawn felt sick of all of it—Angie's mean side, the way the other girls were too scared to stand up to her, the sinking feeling Shawn got whenever she saw Angie glaring at her. Shawn sighed. *I'm not gonna quit cheerleading just because of Angie,* she decided. *I'm not gonna let her win.*

That night, the Moores' house seemed empty without Mom and Dad, who had left for London that afternoon. Aunt Livia seemed to sense that the kids were already missing their parents, and tried to cheer them up by playing the radio loud and making her famous spaghetti sauce with sausage.

"How was school today, everybody?" Aunt Livia asked.

"Fine," the twins said together.

"Matthew?"

"Boring." Matthew pushed his spaghetti around and stared at his plate.

Aunt Livia raised her eyebrows. "Really? All of it was boring? Not one single interesting thing happened?"

Matthew dropped his fork. "I *hate* this spaghetti! Mom never makes it with gross sausage!" He pushed his chair back and ran upstairs to his room.

The twins looked at each other, shocked.

"Goodness," Aunt Livia said lightly. "I was just kidding."

Molly cleared her throat. "I bet he's missing Mom and Dad," she said. "They've never gone away for more than a weekend before." Amanda nodded in agreement.

A concerned look crossed Aunt Livia's face. "Oh, of course! Poor Matthew. I'll go talk to him." She left the table and hurried upstairs after him.

The twins sat in silence for a moment at the big dining room table. "He'll be okay," Molly said finally. "We can take care of him, too. Like, not tease him or boss him around too much."

Amanda nodded. "Definitely. He just needs a day or two to get used to Mom and Dad being away."

Soon, the twins heard laughter coming from upstairs. A few minutes later, Aunt Livia and Matthew returned to the dining room, smiling. Matthew had tear stains on his cheeks, but his sisters didn't mention it.

"So," Aunt Livia said cheerfully, "I will never, ever make spaghetti with sausage again. Really, I don't know what I was thinking." She winked at the twins behind Matthew's back. "I'm just going to get something else for Matthew to eat."

"How about plain spaghetti? We have a jar of spaghetti sauce downstairs in our freezer," Amanda spoke up. "It doesn't have any meat in it."

"Thanks, Manda," Aunt Livia said, moving over to the door that led to the basement. "I'll pay Dish later!"

"Forget it," laughed Amanda. "It's on the house!"

Aunt Livia told lots of funny jokes and stories, and soon even Matthew was cracking up with the twins.

"I've decided that spaghetti wasn't what I really wanted for dinner," Aunt Livia said mischievously after dinner. "What I really wanted was *pizza*."

Amanda and Molly glanced at each other.

Where's she going with this? Molly asked Amanda with her eyes.

No clue, Amanda replied.

"We're gonna order a pizza now?" Matthew asked with wide eyes.

Aunt Livia looked thoughtful. "No...I don't think so. I think we should make one."

"Um, we're not really hungry anymore," Molly spoke up. "Maybe we should make pizza tomorrow night."

"Not hungry? Not hungry for dessert pizza?" Aunt Livia asked, acting surprised. "All right, then, Matthew and I will just eat it all ourselves."

"Awesome!" cheered Matthew.

"Dessert pizza?" asked the twins at the same time.

"Oh, yeah. What *is* dessert pizza, anyway?" Matthew asked.

Aunt Livia grinned. "*Mmm*, it's scrumptious! You'll love it! I thought it would be the perfect dessert tonight...for a special treat."

Aunt Livia showed Molly, Amanda, and Matthew how to mix graham cracker crumbs with sugar and melted butter to make a delicious cookie crust. After they patted the crust into a flat circle on a pizza pan, Aunt Livia got out all sorts of yummy toppings that she'd bought at Choice Foods—miniature marshmallows, chocolate chips, caramels, peanut butter candies. A few minutes later, after everyone helped add the toppings to the dessert pizza, Aunt Livia put it in the oven and baked it for ten minutes. She topped each piece with ice cream and whipped cream.

"*Mmm*, amazing," Amanda sighed after her first bite. "We have to make this for a Chef Girls sleepover. This is, like, the most fantastic dessert *ever*."

"You think every dessert is the most fantastic one *ever*," Molly teased her sister. It was true—Amanda had a serious sweet tooth!

"That's okay, Manda—I'm the same way," Aunt Livia said with a laugh.

Matthew was quiet again—but this time, it was

because his mouth was too full of the gooey, delicious treat to tease his sister!

After school the next day, Amanda hurried to Mr. D.'s classroom for the election meeting. She was eager to find out more about student council—as well as to see who she would be running against for class president.

"Amanda! Early as always," teased Mr. Degregorio, who was talking with another student.

"Hi, Mr. D." Amanda greeted her teacher. But she couldn't take her eyes off the tall guy he was talking to, the one with thick, brown hair that fell across his forehead. *Wow, he's so cute!* she thought, feeling her heart beat a little faster. *How come I haven't seen him around?*

Just then, the guy looked up and saw Amanda staring at him. Before she could help it, a flush crept across her face. *Oh, man, I hope he doesn't think I was checking him out!* she fretted.

"Hey, I'm Evan Anderson," the guy said, coming forward and reaching his hand out to Amanda. "It's Amanda, right?"

"Y-Yes, Amanda Moore," Amanda answered. Evan's warm smile was infectious—she couldn't help grinning back.

"What are you running for?" Evan asked.

His eyes are such a dark blue, Amanda thought. *I've never seen such dark blue eyes before.* "Seventh-grade

42

class president," she answered.

"I was seventh-grade president last year," Evan replied. "It was fantastic! The best part was planning the ski trip. Actually, I had such a great time that this year, I'm running for eighth-grade class president."

"Cool!" Amanda said brightly. "Mr. D. was talking about student council in class the other day—it sounds awesome."

"I had Mr. D. last year, too," Evan said, looking mischievously at the social studies teacher. "Have you had the constitution quiz yet? It was brutal!"

Mr. D. and Amanda laughed. "It wasn't that bad," Mr. D. retorted.

Soon the room was full of students from sixth, seventh, and eighth grade, each excited to find out more about the elections. Amanda spotted a cute, red-headed girl coming in the door.

"Hey, Tessa!" Amanda called, waving the girl over. She and Tessa had become friends when they'd both performed in the school musical *My Fair Lady* the year before.

"Amanda! Hi!" Tessa exclaimed, dropping her backpack on the desk next to Amanda's. "How's everything going? I barely see you these days!"

"I know. I can't believe we don't have any classes together," Amanda replied. "Hey, how come you don't do the plays anymore?"

Tessa shrugged. "I don't know. *My Fair Lady* was fun and all, but I've been trying new things."

"That's cool," Amanda said. "So, what are you running for?" *Oh, I hope she's not running for president,* Amanda thought. *I'd so hate to run against one of my friends.*

"Treasurer," Tessa replied. "Last year, I was treasurer for the ski club. I liked it a lot—I'm really good with numbers and budgets and stuff. What are you running for?"

"President," Amanda replied, feeling relieved.

"Amanda! Molly! Whoever you are—*wassup?*" Amanda looked up to see Omar Kazdan standing nearby.

"Hey, Omar. You know who I am," Amanda couldn't help but smile at goofy Omar and his corny jokes.

"You know I do, Amanda. What are you doing here? The drama club is down the hall, duh."

"I'm running for student council, duh," Amanda joked.

"That's cool. Me, too. Vice president, I think. Something easy, you know? No pressure."

Amanda smiled, shaking her head. Before she could respond, Mr. D. raised his voice above the chattering students.

"Listen up, everybody, let's get started," he called out. "It's great to see so many of you here! Let's start by talking about the different roles and responsibilities of being involved in student council. After that, I'd like to go around the room so you can all introduce yourselves and say what you're running for.

"There are four positions for each grade—president, vice president, secretary, and treasurer. Each class officer is a member of the student council, which meets once a week. Class officers meet twice a month to discuss specific things for their grade, with the president overseeing each meeting. If the president can't attend a meeting, the vice president takes over. The secretary takes notes for each meeting, and the treasurer keeps track of the budget. Any questions? No? Okay, let's start the introductions."

As the students introduced themselves, Amanda looked around the room at all the seventh-graders she knew. *I wonder who else is running for president,* she thought. *What if I'm the only one? That would be awesome—I'd win for sure! But would they let the election happen with just one candidate?*

As if he knew what she was thinking, Evan (who had nabbed a seat next to Amanda in the front) raised his eyebrows and smiled at Amanda. "If you're the only one running, you'll be a shoo-in for sure," he whispered.

Amanda smiled back, trying to look modest and excited at the same time.

The classroom door banged open. Amanda looked up to see who it was—and felt her stomach drop.

Ohmigosh—what is she *doing here?*

"Sorry I'm late!" Angie Martinez said loudly, her hand on her hip. "I completely spaced and thought the meeting was tomorrow!"

"That's okay, Angie," said Mr. Degregorio. "Why don't

you introduce yourself to the rest of the candidates and tell everyone what you're running for."

Angie flashed a bright smile. "Hi, everyone! I'm Angie Martinez—and I'm running for seventh-grade class president!"

chapter 5

To: qtpie490; happyface; BrooklynNatasha
From: mooretimes2
Re: OHMIGOSH!!!

———————————————

Hey, everybody. Molly & Amanda here.
Amanda went 2 the 1ˢᵗ meeting for
student council elections and guess
what? ANGIE IS RUNNING AGAINST HER
FOR CLASS PREZ!!! We're NOT kidding.

If Angie wins, it would be THE
worst thing ever for the 7ᵗʰ grade
class. Now more than ever we need
your help to make sure Amanda wins.
Can U all come to a campaign meeting
at our house tomorrow after school?

Let us know ASAP.

Thanx!!!

M&A

The next afternoon, Molly and Amanda walked home

from school together, stopping at Choice Foods on the way. Peichi, Shawn, and Natasha would be coming over after their after-school activities—and they'd all be hungry. The twins bought pizza sauce, bagels, mozzarella cheese, and yummy pizza toppings—mushrooms, pepperoni, olives, and green pepper.

When the twins got home, Aunt Livia was in the front hall, taking off her coat. "Hi, girls," Aunt Livia said cheerfully. "When are your friends coming over?" She followed Molly and Amanda into the kitchen.

"Around three-thirty," Amanda replied, glancing at the big clock over the kitchen sink. "We're making mini-pizzas for a snack."

"We've eaten pizza with the Chef Girls so many times, we know exactly what everybody likes on their pizza!" Molly laughed.

Just then, Matthew came barreling into the kitchen, carrying a large bag from the Imaginarium Toy Store on Seventh Avenue. "Guess what I got! Guess what I got!" he yelled to the twins.

"We give up. What?"

"*This*!" Matthew exclaimed, pulling a brightly-colored box out of the bag.

"A Barf-o Blender? Gross," said Amanda, examining the box.

"What is it?" Molly asked.

Aunt Livia chuckled. "There's a line of cooking products

for boys—really yucky, disgusting things. So Matthew and I figured, why should girls have all the cooking fun?"

"You can make puke smoothies!" Matthew said excitedly. "And mucous milkshakes!"

"That is truly disgusting," Amanda said, wrinkling her nose. She washed her hands and started grating the cheese.

Meanwhile, Molly placed bagel halves face-up on a baking tray. "Do you guys want some bagel pizzas?" she asked Aunt Livia and Matthew.

"Yeah! Make me four. I mean, five!" Matthew said excitedly, grabbing a black olive out of the colander.

"I think one will be enough," Aunt Livia said with her loud laugh that sounded just like Mom's. "We'll be having dinner in a few hours, after all."

She helped Molly slice the olives and mushrooms and chop the green pepper into tiny cubes. Amanda spooned a couple of tablespoons of pizza sauce on each bagel, and the twins let Matthew sprinkle the grated cheese on top (after he had washed his hands with soap and water!). Then Molly and Amanda topped each pizza with their friends' favorite toppings.

"Shawn loves pepperoni and mushroom...Peichi wants the works...Natasha is olive and green pepper," Amanda murmured. "Matthew is plain, of course. How about you, Aunt Livia?"

"I want a little bit of everything!" Aunt Livia declared.

As Molly slid the tray into the oven, the doorbell rang. "Perfect timing!" she said as Amanda went to let the Chef Girls in.

"Hey, what smells so good?" Peichi asked as she walked into the kitchen.

"Bagel pizzas," Molly answered.

"Awesome!" Peichi cheered.

After the girls finished eating their pizzas, they shooed Matthew out of the kitchen and got to work.

"I have to be home by four-thirty," Natasha said, glancing at her watch. "My mom always wants me to come right home after Hebrew school so I can start my homework, but I convinced her to let me come over for a little while today. I told her it was *urgent*!"

"It is," Amanda said seriously. "There's no way Angie can win. No way!"

Peichi shrugged. "I'm not worried!" she said confidently. "I mean, come on, Amanda. You're the clear choice. No one in their right mind would vote for a wicked witch like Angie."

Amanda shook her head. "She's got the cheerleader-popularity thing going," she replied matter-of-factly.

"Right," Molly chimed in.

Shawn looked down at her plate.

"Whoa! Shawn, I—I totally didn't think about you and Angie being on the cheerleading team," said Amanda, slapping her forehead. "Will it make things really weird if you help on my campaign?"

Shawn shrugged. "Honestly, I don't know. I was a little worried...but the bottom line is that I want *you* to win, Amanda. Also, I told you I would help you with your campaign. Actually, I don't even know if Angie would want my help. We, um, we haven't really talked much since last spring."

The Chef Girls nodded quietly. Each one knew how hard it must have been for Shawn to end her friendship with Angie.

"Okay!" Amanda said, opening a notebook. "First things first. Molly volunteered to be my campaign manager—thanks, Molls!—and last night we made up a list of things we need to do. Take a look."

Amanda ♥ ♥ ♥ ♥ ♥ ♥ ♥ ♥ ♥ ♥ ♥

1. COME UP WITH PLATFORMS
2. MAKE POSTERS
3. FUNNY/GOOD CAMPAIGN SLOGANS—BE CREATIVE!
4. GIMMICKY-THINGIES
5. GET READY FOR THE DEBATE!!!

"So, what are your platforms?" Natasha asked.

"Well, my big one is that I think we all deserve better school lunches," Amanda began. "Yummier food. And healthier, too. Like, I have no idea why the pizzas

51

always have those puddles of grease on them. *Our* pizza doesn't have that." The Chef Girls nodded in agreement, scrunching up their faces as they thought about the super-oily pizzas served in the caf every Friday.

"And I think it would be *awesome* to have a big end-of-the-school-year dance," Amanda continued. "Like, where everyone has to get all dressed up and stuff."

Molly rolled her eyes. "None of the guys will think that's a good idea."

"Maybe they will!" Amanda protested. "Everybody had fun at that dance last Valentine's Day, remember?"

"Those platforms sound good," Natasha said. "Especially the school lunch one. But maybe you should have another serious one, too. Like another way to make the school better, you know?"

Amanda nodded. "That is a good idea." Everyone was quiet for a moment.

"I know!" cried Molly. "A big fundraiser! Like the charity harvest we helped out with for the Windsor Volunteers' Club!"

"That's an *awesome* idea, Molls!" Amanda grinned. "That was a ton of fun. And the school could definitely use the money. Okay—I think three platforms is enough. Do you?"

"Yeah. Next thing: posters," Molly said, glancing at Amanda's list. Before she could continue, Shawn cut her off.

"I'm all over it," she said with a smile. "I have tons of art supplies. Leave it to me!"

"*Oooh*—I was hoping you'd say that!" squealed Amanda. "You're such a great artist, Shawn! The posters will look awesome if you do them! Okay, next—campaign slogans. This one is gonna be tough."

"Natasha, we always have to come up with catchy headlines for *the Post*," Molly said. "We need to do the same thing now!"

"Hey, I've got one!" Peichi exclaimed. "Amanda Moore: She Puts the *Fun* in Fundraiser!"

No one said anything. Amanda smiled weakly.

"You're right, that's pretty lame," Peichi admitted with a smile. "This *is* hard!"

"Here's one!" Natasha said. "Windsor Deserves Moore: Vote for Amanda! Get it? M-O-O-R-E!"

"That's great!" Amanda said with a grin. She wrote it down in the notebook.

"Yeah, your last name is perfect," Shawn said. "How about this for posters about the lunch platform: Moore Delicious, Moore Nutritious—Moore Reasons to Vote for Amanda!"

"I love it!" cried Amanda.

"Hey, maybe I can write an article about you for *the Post*," Natasha spoke up.

"Oh, would you?" Amanda said. "That would be awesome."

"What are 'gimmicky-thingies'?" asked Shawn, glancing at Amanda's list.

53

"That was Molly's idea," Amanda explained. "Funny, creative ideas that would make people remember me and wanna vote for me!"

"We could bake a ton of cookies and write 'Vote for Amanda' on them in frosting!" Molly said. "Since cooking is what we do best!"

"This isn't a gimmick, really, but I think we should make flyers about how qualified Amanda is for the job," Natasha spoke up. "If we have fun things, creative things, *and* concrete reasons, it will be easy to convince people that Amanda's the best candidate."

Suddenly, Amanda's eyes brightened. "You know how everyone says that school elections are just a popularity contest?" she asked excitedly. "Well, let's just embrace that! We could have a party here for our friends in the seventh grade. Kind of making fun of the idea, but getting the word out, too!"

Molly nodded happily. "We haven't had a big party with our other pals since our New Year's brunch," she reminded her twin. "It'll be great! And I'm sure Aunt Livia will let us."

"Okay! The last thing we have to do is discuss the debate," Amanda said, checking her list. "That's the one that makes me nervous. I mean, I've never done anything like that before."

"Yeah, right." Molly rolled her eyes. "Anytime Mom says no, you debate her about it!"

Amanda poked her twin in the arm. "Very funny, Molls. Mr. D. said it was more like giving a speech than debating—like, we're not going head-to-head with the other candidates or anything."

"Amanda, you don't have to worry," Shawn said encouragingly. "You'll be a natural at public speaking!"

"Yeah!" Peichi agreed. "You're great onstage. It's practically the same thing."

"But it's in front of the entire school!" Amanda moaned, burying her face in her hands.

"You know what?" asked Natasha. "Elizabeth is on the debate team. I bet she would help you with it—like, give you some public speaking tips and stuff."

"Perfect," Amanda said gratefully. "I'll call her tonight!"

"*Ohmigosh!*" Natasha exclaimed suddenly. "It's 4:25! I'm gonna have to *run* home or my mom will be seriously mad!"

"I'd better go, too," said Shawn. "My dad and I are cooking dinner tonight and he'll probably be home soon."

"Wait, just one more thing," Amanda said, rummaging through her backpack. "I've got my petition form—I have to get fifty signatures from people who would vote for me, and I want you guys to be the first to sign it!"

"You got it!" Molly said with a grin, grabbing a pen and writing her name in large letters. The rest of the Chef Girls signed after she did.

"Guys, thanks so much for all your help today," said Amanda as she and Molly walked their friends to the door. "See you tomorrow!"

I have the best friends, Amanda thought as she watched Peichi, Shawn, and Natasha walk quickly down Taft Street. She shut the door against the chilly breeze. Even though it was only four-thirty, it was almost dark out.

"Hey, Molls?" Amanda called out. "Do you want to talk more about fun, gimmicky things we can do for my campaign?"

"Actually, Amanda, I was going to plant my basil seeds before dinner," Molly replied from the mudroom.

"Oh, okay," Amanda said, walking toward the mudroom. Molly had five terra-cotta pots lined up on the long table in there. The bag of potting soil had fallen over, scattering dirt all over the table, but Molly was reading the back of the basil seed packet so intently that she hadn't even noticed.

Amanda wandered back to the kitchen to start cleaning up the snack leftovers. Aunt Livia was already there, looking at one of Mom's cookbooks.

"Hey, sweetness," Aunt Livia said. "How was the brainstorming meeting?"

"It was great!" Amanda said happily. "Everyone came up with some awesome ideas. I think the campaign is gonna be so much fun. And, check it out—I already got four signatures on my petition!"

"Good for you!" Aunt Livia said encouragingly. "Getting that petition filled out will be a fabulous opportunity to meet lots of new people in your grade."

"I didn't think of that," Amanda said thoughtfully as she cleared her friends' snack plates off the table. "I was planning to ask people I know—kids I have classes with and stuff."

Aunt Livia shook her head. "Part of a successful campaign is meeting new people, introducing yourself, telling them why you're the best candidate for the job. The petition is a great chance to get started on that!"

"You're right," Amanda said, nodding. "Eek, though—I hate just walking up to people and introducing myself! I always feel shy and kind of...I don't know, stupid or something."

"Oh, but you shouldn't, sweetie," Aunt Livia said quickly. "What do you think when someone walks up to you and introduces herself? I always think, 'Wow, this person is really confident!' And it's also flattering when someone else makes the effort to meet you, you know? It'll show the other kids that you're interested in them—and their opinions."

"That's so true," said Amanda. "Thanks, Aunt Livia!"

"That's what aunts are for," Aunt Livia said cheerfully. "And do you know what nieces are for? Making delicious green salads to go with dinner."

"That's something I can definitely handle," Amanda replied.

As the twins helped Aunt Livia do the dishes after dinner, Amanda remembered something. "Oh, Aunt Livia!" she exclaimed. "Would it be okay if Molly and I have a party in a couple weeks? Right before the election? We'd invite, like, fifteen people from our grade. And we'll make all the food and clean up, of course."

Aunt Livia's eyes twinkled. "I don't see why not," she said. "But I'm happy to help with the cooking!"

"Thanks so much! It's going to be fantastic!" Amanda said excitedly.

A few minutes later, Amanda and Molly went to the den to send an e-vite about their party.

"Shawn, Peichi, Natasha, Justin, Omar, Tessa...um, Elizabeth...Connor, of course," Amanda thought out loud. "That's eight. Who else should we invite?"

Molly scrunched up her nose. "I'm not really sure," she said. "Those are our closest friends in seventh grade. Hey, maybe we could just write 'bring a friend,' and get some new people at our party who we don't know very well!"

"Good idea!" Amanda agreed. She started typing.

To: BrooklynNatasha; qtpie490; happyface; justmac; cookincon11; octoberfaerie; cheerbaby; funnyomy478
From: mooretimes2
Re: PARTY! PARTY! PARTY!

Hey Everybody,

Your fave twins here, Molly and Amanda. We're having a big party for Amanda, since she's running for 7th grade class prez. And you're all invited!

Date: Saturday in 2 weeks
Time: 6:30, 7:00—whenever you get here!
Place: Our place! (Need directions? Call us!)
Bring: A pal! Help spread the word about . . .

AMANDA FOR PRESIDENT!!!

See you soon!!!
Molly & Amanda

"That ought to do it," Amanda said, reading over the invitation. "We've got all the important stuff down there."

Molly nodded. "Let's send it. This is gonna be fun!"

59

The next morning, Amanda got to homeroom before the first bell, ready to ask the other students there to sign her petition—some of whom she'd never really spoken to before. To her surprise, Angie—who was always late—was already there, standing next to Erica Mackenzie's desk.

Shoot! Amanda thought angrily. *Angie got here early to get signatures for her petition. Erica's really nice, too—I bet she would have signed mine.*

Molly leaned over to Amanda. "I guess you were right to be worried about Angie, Manda," she whispered. "Looks like she really wants to win."

"Well, so do I," Amanda whispered back. "Angie is *not* just gonna walk away with this election." She dropped her bag on her desk, pulled out her petition and a pen, and walked over to Paul Mellon, a quiet red-haired seventh-grader with glasses.

"Oh, hey, Amanda, what's up?" Paul asked quickly.

He looks so surprised to see me, Amanda thought. She cleared her throat. "Um, hi, Paul," she began. "Uh, how are you?"

"I'm good," Paul said, still looking completely

surprised that Amanda had come over to talk to him.

"I'm, um, running for seventh-grade class president, and I was hoping you'd sign my petition," Amanda began. She took a deep breath. "I've got some great ideas for ways to make Windsor Middle School better." As she gave Paul details about her platforms, Amanda slowly began to feel more sure of herself. "...And I'd love to hear any ideas you have for making Windsor better, too," she finished.

"School lunches are really gross!" Paul said with a smile. "If you can make 'em better, you've definitely got my vote."

"Thanks!" Amanda said happily as Paul signed her petition. *Five signatures done...forty-five more to go!*

By lunchtime, Amanda had collected another six signatures for her petition—but she still had a long way to go. She scarfed down her lunch and was done eating by the time Shawn got out of the lunch line.

"Whoa! Where are you heading?" Shawn asked as she put her tray down on the long cafeteria table.

"Gotta get more signatures. The petition is due by the end of the day Monday and I don't want Angie getting to everybody before me."

"Manda, wait," Molly called. "Are you free this afternoon? I have to cover the Windsor football game for *the Post* and if you come with me, you could get some of the kids in the bleachers to sign, too."

"Great idea, Molls," Amanda said, nodding her head. "Plus, if kids see me at a football game, they'll know I really am interested in everybody and everything at Windsor. See ya after school!"

Molly smiled as she watched her twin start working the cafeteria, thinking, *Wow! She's become a real politician already!*

After school, Amanda met Molly at her locker and the twins walked over to the football field together.

"I got eight more signatures for my petition this afternoon," Amanda chattered. "Now I only need thirty-one more and I'm done! I might even be able to hand it in early!"

"Great," Molly said as they reached the field. Peichi had already staked out a spot on the bleachers, and was waving wildly to get the twins' attention.

"Hey, here come the cheerleaders! Shawn's right in front. She's doing so awesome this year!"

"It's so cool that Coach Carson made Shawn a center front after cheerleading camp. Usually, an eighth-grader gets that position!" Molly added.

The twins and Peichi looked down at the field,

where the cheerleaders were arranging themselves for an opening cheer. Shawn looked amazing in her red-and-white cheerleading uniform. Her eyes sparkled and she seemed full of energy.

"Hey, Amanda! What's up?"

Amanda turned around to see who was calling her.

It was Evan!

And he was climbing the bleachers toward her!

"Hey, Evan," Amanda called back, feeling her heart start to beat a little faster. "You came to the game?" *Duh!* she thought. *Of course he came to the game!* Amanda felt her cheeks flush.

"You bet. I love football. How about you?" Evan sat down on the bench next to Amanda.

Ohmigosh! Is he really gonna sit here—right next to me? "Yeah. I mean, football's okay. I don't watch it on TV or anything, but I like going to Windsor sports and stuff," Amanda replied. *Okay! That was a little better!* She cleared her throat. "I also thought I'd get some signatures for my petition."

"Good thinking! I should do the same thing," he said. Amanda noticed how his deep blue eyes were flecked with brown and grey.

"So, how many signatures do you have?" Evan asked.

"Nineteen," Amanda answered. "How about you?"

"Wow, that's really good for the first day!" Evan replied, sounding impressed. "I've got thirty-two. I try to get the signatures as soon as possible, so the opposition doesn't beat me to it, you know?"

Amanda laughed. "That's exactly what I'm trying to do!"

"Evan! Hey, Evan!" called a boy who was sitting with a group of eighth-graders. "What's up, man?"

"Hey, Josh!" Evan called back. He turned to Amanda. "I've gotta run. I don't have signatures from any of them yet!" he said. "It was good talking to you, Amanda. See ya later." Evan bounded up the bleachers toward the group of eighth-graders. Amanda heard loud laughter coming from the kids. *He's so popular,* she thought. *Evan must know, like, the entire school.* She turned around to see Molly and Peichi looking at her.

"What?" she asked.

"Who was *that*? He's really *cute*!" Peichi exclaimed in a loud whisper. As Amanda burst into giggles and tried to shush Peichi, Molly rolled her eyes.

"His name is Evan Anderson and he's on student council," said Amanda. "He *is* really cute, isn't he!"

"You missed, like, the entire routine," Molly pointed out. "Shawn did great."

Down on the field, the cheerleaders finished their opening cheer and the referee blew a whistle, signaling the start of the game. Molly quickly got out her notebook and a pen to take notes for her article.

A few minutes into the game, Amanda lost track of how the two teams were playing. She tried to turn around discreetly to see what Evan was doing with his friends. He'd moved on to another group of kids and was getting more signatures for his petition. *I should get some signatures, too,* she thought. Glancing around the bleachers, Amanda noticed Justin and Connor sitting together.

"Be right back," she told Molly and Peichi. She walked over to Justin, who was taking pictures of the game for *the Post.* "Hey, guys," she said, trying to sound as confident as Evan. "What's going on?"

"Not much," Justin replied distractedly as he focused the camera on Windsor's quarterback. Connor was so wrapped up in the game that he didn't even answer.

Amanda watched the game in silence with the boys for a few minutes, waiting for a break so she could ask them to sign her petition. Finally, the ref blew a whistle to signal the end of the first quarter.

"Wow! What a great start!" Justin exclaimed, putting his camera on his lap.

"It's a really good game," Amanda agreed, hoping that Justin wouldn't ask her any questions about the first quarter, since she'd barely been paying attention. She cleared her throat. "Um, I'm running for seventh-grade class president, and I was wondering if you guys would sign my petition," she said with a big smile, trying to sound upbeat and confident.

Justin smiled at Amanda with his slow, easy grin. "I'd love to," he said. "But I can't. I already signed Omar's petition this morning. He asked first. But I'll definitely come to your party in a couple weeks. Sounds really fun."

Connor nodded in agreement.

"But—but Omar's running for vice president," replied Amanda, confused. "That's what he said at the meeting. So you can still sign mine."

Justin shook his head. "He must have changed his mind, 'cause his petition definitely said 'president' on it. And he was talking on and on about it—he's got a ton of crazy ideas. You know Omar!"

Amanda nodded, too surprised to reply.

"But good luck, Amanda! You and Omar—that'll be a really good race. I know that—*run! Run! Run!*" Justin suddenly shouted as he jumped to his feet and started snapping pictures. Amanda glanced down at the field, where Windsor's quarterback was dashing across the grass, trying to land a touchdown.

"Score!" Justin yelled, giving Connor a high five. "All right!"

"Okay, thanks a lot," Amanda mumbled. "See you later."

"Uh-huh," said Justin, peering through his camera lens. Connor was still clapping.

"Hey! What's the matter? Wouldn't Justin sign your petition?" Peichi asked Amanda when she saw Amanda's grim expression.

Amanda shook her head. "No. And guess why? Because he already signed Omar's petition. For class president!

Can you believe it? *Omar Kazdan* for class president!"

Peichi's eyes grew wide, then she burst out laughing. "No way! I had no idea Omar was running. But don't worry, Manda. You'll totally beat him."

Molly nodded in agreement. "Yeah, Omar's such a goofball, no one will take him seriously for class president, anyway."

Amanda shrugged. "Thanks, guys. I was just... surprised. Beating Angie was gonna be hard enough... but beating Omar *and* Angie..."

Molly briefly put her arm around her twin. "No worries, Manda! You're still the best candidate. I know you'll rock the election."

Amanda smiled at her sister, but, inside, she wasn't so sure.

chapter 7

After the game, the cheerleaders walked across the field back to the locker room to change. Shawn was tired—but she was still pumped.

"You were so great, Shawn," Jenn said as Shawn twirled the dial on her combination lock.

"Thanks," Shawn replied with a smile.

"Did you hear that Angie is running for class president?" Ashley spoke up. "Wouldn't that be so awesome, to have a cheerleader as class president?"

As the girls around her agreed, Shawn got ready to take off her cheerleading uniform and slip into her top in one quick movement. *I hate changing in front of everyone,* Shawn thought. *I shouldn't have worn the turtleneck. It's always harder to put on than a regular shirt.*

"So, Shawn, are you free this afternoon?" Ashley asked, pulling Shawn back to the conversation.

"Huh? For what?" Shawn asked, slipping her arms out of her uniform. *I just wanna change,* she thought. *Could we please have this conversation later?*

"We're going over to Angie's apartment to help her with her campaign," repeated Ashley. "All the seventh-grade cheerleaders are going. Can you come?"

"Um, no, I don't think so," Shawn replied in a muffled voice as she tried to pull her turtleneck over her head. Her cheerleading top fell to the floor.

"Yeah, it is kind of late," agreed Jenn. "How about tomorrow after school?"

Shawn shook her head as she hopped into her jeans. "Sorry."

"Look, Shawn," Ashley said in a serious tone. "We know you and Angie had a big fight. But can't you just put it behind you? This is a really big deal. We should all stick together and help Angie get elected!"

"I can't," Shawn said. "I already promised Amanda that I would help on her campaign. And I can't really work on two campaigns at once, you know?"

Ashley and Jenn looked shocked. Then Jenn cleared her throat. "Shawn, Amanda's sister can help her out. But this is for the *squad*."

Shawn started feeling frustrated. *How does Angie being class president help the squad?* she thought. But she kept her voice even as she replied, "Sorry, guys, but I'm not gonna go back on my word. Besides, you'll all be great on Angie's campaign." She stuffed her uniform and cheerleading shoes into her gym bag. "See ya!" she called out as she slung the bag over her shoulder.

The other cheerleaders were quiet. Then Jenn called, "Bye, Shawn." But Ashley didn't even say good-bye.

Outside the locker room, Shawn took a deep breath.

She had no regrets about her decision to help Amanda. But somewhere deep inside her, she knew that she'd crossed a line. *I wonder if everyone on the squad will start treating me different now—just like Angie does?*

With the school play happening on Thursday and Friday nights, Amanda was so busy that Molly felt like she barely saw her. On Saturday morning, though, both twins woke up early.

Molly yawned and stretched as she sat up in bed. "Morning, Manda," she mumbled.

"Morning, Molls," Amanda said back with a smile. "It's so early—and quiet! I don't think anyone else is up yet. Hey! Let's go downstairs and make breakfast for Aunt Livia and Matthew!"

"Good idea," Molly said as she climbed out of bed and pulled on her cozy flannel bathrobe.

Fifteen minutes later, the twins had whipped up a batch of Dad's delicious blueberry pancakes. Amanda was heating milk in a small pot to make cocoa for Matthew, Molly, and herself, while Molly was trying to figure out the coffeemaker.

"It *should* be easy," she said, staring at the machine. "I mean, Dad is practically still asleep when he makes the coffee every morning!"

"You need a filter," Amanda said over her shoulder as she heated up the griddle. "They're in the cupboard next to the sink. You put the filter and the coffee in the thing at the top, and the water drips through and that makes the coffee."

"Thanks!" Molly said. "How do *you* know how to make coffee?"

"I'm always more awake than you are in the mornings!" Amanda teased her sister. "I actually notice what goes on around me."

"Okay, if you know so much, tell me this," Molly teased back. "How much coffee do I use?" She opened the container of coffee. "There's a little scoop in here."

"I'm not sure," Amanda admitted as she flicked tiny droplets of water on the griddle to see if it was hot enough. When the water droplets sizzled and danced on the griddle's smooth surface, she carefully ladled some pancake batter on it. "It's probably like how it is for hot chocolate—one scoop per cup."

"That makes sense," Molly reasoned. "I think Aunt Livia usually has two or three cups of coffee in the morning. But I'll use four, just in case she wants more."

Soon, the kitchen was filled with delicious smells of sweet cocoa, fluffy pancakes, warm maple syrup, and brewing coffee. The twins hated the taste of coffee, but they always thought it smelled wonderful.

Aunt Livia and Matthew came into the kitchen as Molly and Amanda were setting the table. "Wow! Did you girls do all this? What a treat!" Aunt Livia exclaimed, glancing around.

"Surprise!" yelled the twins at the same time.

"Hot chocolate! Awesome!" Matthew cheered, rushing to the table.

"And coffee—just what I need," Aunt Livia said gratefully as she poured herself a big cup.

After the twins placed a tall platter of pancakes on the table, everyone sat down to eat.

"These pancakes are fab," Aunt Livia complimented the twins after her first bite. She smiled as she took a big sip of her coffee. Suddenly, her smile faded and her eyes grew wide as she swallowed hard. Though she tried to hide it, a grimace crossed her face.

"What is it? What's wrong?" Amanda asked.

Aunt Livia gulped. "Wow! That is some *strong* coffee!" she said, her loud laugh making the kids smile. "How much coffee grounds did you use?"

"Just four scoops," Molly replied. "Is that too much?"

Aunt Livia nodded. "You only need one or two. But that's okay! With some milk and sugar, this will be perfect. It'll be a café au lait—like they drink in New Orleans!"

The twins grinned at each other as they did the "twin thing" again, thinking, *Oops! Guess there are still some things about cooking we have to learn!*

"So what's everyone up to today?" Aunt Livia asked after she fixed her coffee.

"Elizabeth is coming over to coach me for the debate," said Amanda. "And tonight's the last night of the play. You guys are coming, right?"

"Of course!" replied Molly. "And the Chef Girls are, too."

"Molly, what are you doing today?"

"I'm going to bottle my pesto sauce and try selling it."

"Fantastic!" Aunt Livia said brightly. "If you're going to start pounding the pavement today, maybe you should practice a sales pitch this morning. Matthew and I are going to the Brooklyn Children's Museum this afternoon with Ben, but I'd be happy to listen to your speech before we leave."

"Me, too—Elizabeth isn't coming over until eleven-thirty," Amanda spoke up.

"Thanks—that will be really helpful," Molly replied gratefully.

After breakfast, Aunt Livia and Amanda helped Molly with her sales pitch while they cleaned the kitchen. Then Aunt Livia and Matthew got ready to leave, and Molly started lining up the ingredients for her pesto.

"I thought you were going to use basil you grew yourself," Amanda commented as she watched Molly take several bunches of basil out of the fridge.

"I was, I mean, I am," replied Molly. "But it actually takes a long time to grow. There are, like, tiny little shoots springing up, but it might not be big enough to harvest for two months! And I don't want to wait *that* long to get things going."

Amanda nodded. "Makes sense. Um, do you want me to help or anything?" she asked.

"No, that's okay. It's just pesto. I could make it blindfolded!" Molly joked. She opened a cupboard where she'd been keeping her glass jars. "I sterilized the jars last night, so really all I have to do is make the pesto and pour it into the bottles! I might even walk around Seventh Avenue this afternoon and start selling it!"

Amanda smiled at how excited Molly was about the pesto business. "Okay. I'm going to shower and get ready," Amanda said. "Unless, um, you want to shower first."

Molly looked down at her pajamas and laughed. "Good idea! I guess I should start my business fully dressed!"

A few hours later, Amanda and Elizabeth were holed up in the twins' room, practicing for the debate, while Molly prepared batch after batch of pesto sauce. The phone rang.

"Hello?" Molly answered as she poured her sixth batch of pesto into a tall jar.

"Hi-eeee, Molly! It's Peichi! What are you doing?"

"I'm making pesto for my business," Molly replied.

"Oh! That's really great! Am I interrupting you? Don't worry, I'll be really quick! I just had a question about going to the play tonight. Are we meeting at your house? Or at the auditorium? And what time?" Peichi paused to take a deep breath.

Molly laughed. "We're meeting here at six-thirty," she said. "Then we'll go over early with Amanda."

"Okay! See you then! Good luck with the pesto! Byeeeeee!" Peichi hung up. Five minutes later, the phone rang again.

"Hello?" Molly answered, wondering why Amanda wasn't grabbing the phone like she usually did. *She and Elizabeth must be working really hard,* Molly figured.

"Hi-eeee! It's me, Peichi. Again! Can I come by in a little bit? Just for a few minutes? Are you leaving to sell your pesto right away?"

"I'll probably leave here around two or two-thirty," she said. "So you can drop by any time before that."

"Cool! See you in a few!"

Thirty minutes later, the doorbell rang. It was Peichi and her mom, who was carrying a large manila folder.

"Come on in," Molly said, holding the door open wide. "Hi, Mrs. Cheng. Um, how are you, uh, feeling?" she asked awkwardly, noticing Mrs. Cheng's round belly.

"Pretty good," Mrs. Cheng replied. "I'm not as tired as I

was last month. In fact, I almost have *too* much energy!"

"Seriously," agreed Peichi. "She cleaned out, like, the entire basement yesterday."

"Oh! Can I take your coats?" Molly asked, remembering her manners for once.

Mrs. Cheng shook her head, smiling graciously. "We just dropped by for a minute, Molly," she said.

"Yeah! We have a little surprise for you!" Peichi exclaimed excitedly. "My mom made it! But it was my idea! I hope you like it!"

Mrs. Cheng handed Molly the manila folder. Inside, Molly found labels of all shapes and sizes, each one reading, "Molly's Amazing Pesto Sauce! All Proceeds Donated to Charity! Take a bite...out of hunger!"

"*Ohmigosh!* This is so fantastic!" Molly exclaimed, flipping through the professional-looking labels with their funky designs. "I hadn't even thought about labels. But these are *perfect*! Thank you *so* much!" Mrs. Cheng was a graphic designer. She had designed the cool business card for Dish—and these labels looked just as great.

Peichi clapped her hands happily. "Yay! Way to go, Mom!"

Mrs. Cheng grinned and put her arm around Peichi. "Way to go, Peichi—it was a great idea. And way to go, Molly—this is a fantastic thing you're doing. I'm so impressed!"

Molly blushed. "I just want to, you know, do what I can."

"Well, you're doing great! All of you girls are!" Mrs. Cheng beamed. "I'm really proud of all of you!" She dug in her pocket and pulled out a tissue, then wiped her eyes. "Sorry," she said, smiling through tears. "It's the baby. My emotions are all over the place!" She and Peichi laughed.

"Well, things will be back to normal soon enough," joked Molly. "In five more months, right?"

"Normal?" snorted Peichi.

"Five more months," replied Mrs. Cheng, nodding. "And I hope you'll baby-sit for us sometimes, Molly. I hear you're a wonder with kids!"

"Yeah, and I bet I'll need a break from big sister duty sometimes," Peichi cracked.

"Thanks so much for making these great labels," Molly said to Peichi and Mrs. Cheng again. "They're perfect."

"See you in a few hours!" Peichi waved as she and her mom walked back to their car.

Molly grinned as she closed the door, then hurried back to the kitchen to apply the labels to her jars of pesto.

This looks so professional, Molly thought proudly. *My pesto business is a real thing! I'm gonna get out there right now...and make some money for people who need help!*

chapter 8

"Sorry, we're not looking for any bottled pesto products right now."

Molly tried not to sigh. "Okay," she said. "Let me know if—" But the shopkeeper had already turned his back to help a customer. Molly headed quickly out of the store—the ninth store to turn her down!

It doesn't make sense, Molly thought miserably as she shifted the heavy box in her arms. *Why don't these people want to help the hungry? Don't they understand how important this is?*

Around First Street, Molly decided to walk just a few more blocks south, then go home. Even through her gloves, her fingers were growing numb from the cold weather, and the pale sunlight was fading as an early dusk fell over Brooklyn. She sighed, then pushed open the door of Park Terrace Gourmet, a tiny food store where Mrs. Moore often purchased gift baskets for friends.

"Hello, dear, may I help you?" asked a kindly-looking woman who was sitting on a tall stool behind the counter. "Why don't you put that heavy box down?"

Molly smiled gratefully and put the box on the counter. "Hi, my name is Molly Moore, and I've got something great here," she began, reciting the sales pitch she had practiced with Amanda and Aunt Livia. "Imagine being able to take a bite out of hunger while taking a bite of the best pesto you've ever tasted! Now anyone can—thanks to Molly's Amazing Pesto Sauce. All of the profits go to local food banks. Your customers will keep coming back for more, feeling satisfied that they're helping those in need...and wanting second helpings of this delicious sauce! Would you like to try some? I have some crackers."

The shopkeeper smiled at Molly and pulled a bottle of pesto out of the box. "My, this is awfully ambitious of you!" she said cheerfully. "This pesto looks rich and flavorful. Nice label—very artistic. Where is the expiration date?"

Molly blinked. For a moment, she was speechless. "Um, I forgot to put an expiration date on the bottle," she admitted as her heart sank. "But it lasts for about a week in the fridge."

The woman nodded. "And do you have a list of the ingredients? Some people have allergies and like to check what's in the products they buy."

I feel so dumb, Molly thought. *I never thought of that, either. This lady won't take the pesto. I can already tell.*

As if she could tell how discouraged Molly was, the shopkeeper reached out and patted Molly's arm. "Sit down, dear. You look like you could use a hot cup of tea. My name is Lillian, by the way." She leaned behind her to plug in a small electric kettle.

"Thanks," Molly said sadly. "I—I really wanted to do this pesto business and help out the hungry. It's something I think about so much—families not having enough food, little kids going to sleep hungry..." A lump formed in Molly's throat—partly from exhaustion, partly from frustration—and she took a deep breath to keep from crying as she continued. "I went to, like, ten stores today—and no one was interested."

Lillian smiled kindly. "Selling foodstuffs is very hard!" she began. "There's a lot of liability—risk—for storekeepers. Imagine what would happen if we sold a product that made someone sick. That's why we have to be so careful. Especially with small businesses—most store owners will want to see certification from the Board of Health that proves the food is being made in a sanitary, professional space. And with home-jarred goods, there can be a higher risk of botulism. That's probably why most people turned you down, Molly."

Molly nodded. *I never even thought of all that stuff,* she admitted to herself.

"But I'm sure everyone you spoke to today was just as impressed as I was," Lillian continued, handing Molly a cup of warm ginger tea. Molly took a sip of the sweet, spicy tea and immediately felt warmer inside...and a little happier, too. "You're young, Molly! With your ambition and good heart, I'll bet that

ten years from now, you could have your very own professional pesto bottling plant. You know, the actor Paul
Newman has a line of food products, and he donates the
profits to charities. It's incredibly successful, and I know
yours will be, too—someday. But for now—have fun with
your friends! There's plenty of time for you to make a
difference in the world."

Molly smiled at Lillian. "Thanks for explaining all of
that," she said, and finished her tea. "And thanks for the tea.
My mom likes to shop here, so I'm sure I'll be back soon."

"I look forward to it," Lillian said. "Good luck, Molly!"

Everything Lillian said makes sense, Molly thought as
she trudged back up Seventh Avenue toward home. *But
how can I just abandon my business now? I haven't
helped anyone.*

"Hey! How did it go?" Amanda asked eagerly as she
opened the door for Molly. But one look at her twin's face
told Amanda that the answer was "not good." As Molly told
Amanda about her unsuccessful afternoon, the expression
on Amanda's face changed from one of concern to one of
anger.

"*Oooh,* I *hate* it when people act like kids can't do
things!" Amanda exclaimed.

Molly shook her head. "No, I don't think that's

what Lillian meant," she said thoughtfully. "I think she was trying to say that a packaged food business is too much for kids. Like, kids can't practice medicine, even if they really want to and think it's really important and interesting."

Amanda grinned at her twin. "Well, you're taking it better than I would," Amanda said honestly. "I'd probably be having a fit right now!" The twins giggled. "Come on, Molls. I know exactly what you need—a nice hot bath. I've got some awesome new bubble bath, too—it's jasmine-scented. *Mmm!*"

An hour later, when the Chef Girls arrived to go to the play, Molly felt like a different person. She was completely relaxed from the soothing bath and couldn't wait to spend the evening with her best friends.

Shawn's dad dropped her off first. When Amanda opened the door, she was surprised to see Shawn holding a big stack of posters.

"Hey, Shawn, what's that?" Amanda asked. Then she squealed. "*Ohmigosh!* Are those my campaign posters? Did you make them already? Oh, wow! *Molly! Aunt Livia!* Come here and see this!"

Shawn beamed as Amanda spread the posters all over the dining room table. Shawn had made ten different posters, each decorated with sequins or glitter and big, eye-catching letters and bright, funky designs.

"Oh, Shawn!" breathed Amanda. "These are gorgeous! This must have taken you *forever!*"

Shawn nodded. "I did one each day after school this week, and the rest today," she explained. "I'm so glad you like them."

"Like them? I love them! After the election I'm gonna put them up in my room!"

"What are you putting up in *our* room?" Molly teased as she joined the girls. Then she saw the posters. "Amanda Moore—Moore Experience, Moore Ideas, Moore for 7th Grade Class President!" Shawn, these are outstanding! You are so talented. You should be, like, a famous artist when you grow up!"

Shawn shrugged off the compliment. "You guys..." she said modestly. But inside, she did feel proud. "Manda, you look so cool," she added, changing the subject.

"The crew has to wear all black," Amanda explained, looking down at her black pants and fuzzy black sweater. "And no accessories! I feel so plain."

"No, you look totally sophisticated," Shawn assured her. "Very Manhattan."

"That's what I said," added Aunt Livia as she entered the dining room, wiping her hands on a dishtowel. "Wow! Gorgeous posters, Shawn! I am *very* impressed!"

"Thanks," Shawn said again. "I thought that the rest of us could put them up tonight, since we're getting to school an hour before the play starts."

"It all feels so, I don't know, *real* now," Amanda said quietly. "I'm running for seventh-grade class president!"

"And there's no going back now," Molly joked.

"Definitely not," Amanda agreed, feeling a chill run down her spine.

By Monday afternoon, all of the candidates had their posters up, and the election was heating up. The halls of Windsor Middle School had never looked so colorful—or been so full of corny puns. Amanda felt proud every time she saw one of the beautiful posters Shawn had worked so hard on. They were the best-looking posters by far.

It seemed that the other students were getting excited about the election, too. The debate was in two days, and the school was abuzz with opinions about who would win.

After school, Molly met up with Natasha for a *Post* meeting.

"I'm going to ask Ms. Zane about writing an article on Amanda after the meeting," Natasha said.

"I bet there will be a lot of talk about the election at today's meeting," Molly replied.

Molly was right. Soon after she called the meeting to order, Liza Pedersen, the editor, brought up the elections.

"Paul Verrier and I are going to cover the debate on Wednesday," Liza said. "In case it gets too fast-paced, we'll have a tape recorder going. We should also have a 'fast facts' column where we list each candidate's platform, so students can easily compare and contrast them. Who wants to do that?"

Grace Everett raised her hand.

"Thanks, Grace. Now who wants to cover photography for the debates? Justin? Super," Liza continued. "And you've all been working on the regular columns, right? Great. Deadline is Thursday afternoon at three. Thanks, everybody! E-mail me if you have any questions or problems."

As the students filed out of the newspaper office, Natasha approached Liza and Ms. Zane. "Um, I had an idea for an article about the elections," Natasha began. Ms. Zane nodded encouragingly. "One of my friends, Amanda Moore, is running for seventh-grade class president, and I thought I could write an article on her. She has experience with her own cooking business that really ties into her platform. Um, what do you think?"

Liza and Ms. Zane glanced at each other. "I like your idea," Ms. Zane began. "However, it's important for a newspaper to be fair and impartial, especially in the area of politics. If you wrote an article just about Amanda, it would seem like *the Post* is endorsing her. The other candidates would be upset—and rightfully so. The only way we could have a feature article on one candidate is to have features on each presidential candidate."

85

"I do like that idea, though," Liza spoke up. "We could have one person from each grade write short features on that class's presidential candidates. Natasha, do you think you have time to write articles on Amanda as well as..." Liza paused as she glanced at her notebook. "Omar Kazdan and Angie Martinez?"

Natasha swallowed hard. *No way!* she thought rapidly. *I don't want to go anywhere near Angie. What a disaster that would be! I can't do the article if I have to interview her.* She took a deep breath. "Um, I'm not sure," she replied. "Interviewing three people and writing the article by Thursday afternoon sounds like too much." *Good save!* she congratulated herself.

Liza nodded understandingly. "That's okay," she said. "It *is* a lot. And it might be hard for us to find sixth- and eighth-graders who have the time to report on the candidates for their grades. But it was a great idea, Natasha, and maybe you can work it out for next year's election."

"Okay. Thanks a lot." Natasha grabbed her backpack and headed out of the newspaper office, where Molly was waiting for her.

"How did it go? Are you gonna write an article on Amanda?" Molly asked eagerly.

Natasha shook her head. "I'm sorry, Molly. I really blew it!" She explained how she couldn't bear to interview Angie. "Do you think Amanda's going to be mad at me?"

"I don't think so," Molly said. "You tried. I mean, no

one I know would want to interview Angie, so they can't blame you for that! Besides, it sounds like the candidates are already going to be featured in the paper, with the platform profiles and all."

Natasha smiled at Molly, glad her friend was being so supportive. *I just hope Amanda understands the way Molly does,* Natasha thought.

While Molly and Natasha were attending the *Post* meeting, Shawn was sweating through a tough cheer-leading practice. The first basketball game of the season was that Friday night, and Coach Carson had several indoor routines she wanted the squad to master. By the end of the powerful workout, Shawn felt great—pumped and ready for anything. It wasn't even bothering her that Angie was back on the squad.

Wow, practice went long today, Shawn thought as she checked her watch back in the locker room. *Dad might be home already!* She hurried as she changed, eager to get home and help her dad make dinner. After Shawn's mother had died of a long illness a few years before, Shawn sometimes felt like her dad was all she had. Now they were closer than ever—though sometimes, she still missed her mother so much that it hurt.

Shawn was the first one out of the locker room.

"Bye, everyone," she called over her shoulder. "See you tomorrow!" No one had mentioned helping with Angie's campaign since the other day, and Shawn was glad that they seemed to have dropped it.

"Shawn. Wait up," called a familiar voice as Shawn left.

Shawn's heart sank. "What's up, Angie?" she asked.

"I want to talk to you. I was looking for you all day, girlfriend!" Angie said in that super-friendly tone that used to make Shawn feel like she was Angie's best friend. Angie's dark brown eyes seemed warm and happy, not harsh and hateful as they had recently.

Shawn could hear her heart pounding. "You found me," she said, trying to sound light and jokey.

"Listen, Shawn," Angie began. "I feel really bad about this stupid fight we've been having. I don't even know how it started—that's how lame this fight is. We should just put it behind us. Now that I'm back on the squad, we'll be having all those great times again—just like last year."

"Cool. Are you, um, excited about being back on the squad?" Shawn asked, trying to avoid the issue of their old friendship. *I don't want to be your friend again,* Shawn thought firmly. *I have no interest in that.*

"Totally! And I'm excited about the elections next week. You know I'm running for seventh-grade class president, right?" Angie asked, raising an eyebrow and shooting a piercing look at Shawn.

"Yeah, I heard that," Shawn said, trying to be noncommittal.

"That's one thing I wanted to talk to you about. Shawn, I would so love it if you would help with the campaign. You're *so* smart and creative. We could have a blast! And when I win, everybody in seventh grade will treat us like we're all important. It'll be great!"

So that's what this is all about, Shawn thought angrily. *Angie doesn't care about being my friend—she just wants to use me. I should have known.* Before she knew it, Shawn snapped, "No, Angie. I'm not gonna help with your campaign. I already told Jenn and Ashley that I was helping Amanda."

The warmth in Angie's eyes faded instantly. "*What* is your problem, Shawn?" she spat. "Are you too *good* to help me out? You didn't used to be stuck-up. But now, that's all anyone talks about. Stuck-up Shawn."

"Just leave me alone, Angie!" Shawn yelled. "I can't be your friend after what you did to Elizabeth last year. That was horrible! I don't want to be friends with anyone who could do something like that."

"*Ohmigosh,* Shawn, you don't actually believe I did that," Angie protested, rolling her eyes. "Elizabeth just told Coach that to keep me out of camp. Everybody knows that."

"Do you *ever* stop lying? I *saw* you, Angie! I *saw* you do it!"

Shawn's hand flew up to her mouth. She hadn't meant to say that. For months, Shawn had worried about what would happen if Angie ever learned that Shawn had reported her.

Now, she would find out.

Angie took a step back. Her silence scared Shawn more than if Angie had started shouting. Instead, Angie nodded slowly—as if everything suddenly made sense— and a wicked smile spread across her face.

"You'll pay, Shawn. You'll pay." Angie spoke so softly that Shawn wasn't sure if she'd heard her correctly. But there was no mistaking the rage in Angie's trembling voice. Angie spun around on her heel and stormed down the hall.

A terrible feeling of dread crept over Shawn. *I went too far,* she thought miserably. *Now Angie knows that I told on her. Why couldn't she just leave me alone?* An image flashed into Shawn's mind of Angie stealing Elizabeth's shoes to keep her out of the meet—and then destroying them afterwards. *She made Elizabeth pay, and Elizabeth never even did anything to her...what will she do to me?*

chapter 9

Every day, Amanda spent hours working on her speech for the debate. But the more she worked, the more nervous she became, throwing away draft after draft. Finally, Tuesday night, Amanda walked into the living room where Molly, Aunt Livia, and Matthew were watching TV. She flopped down into a big armchair and sighed heavily.

"What's wrong, Manda?" Molly asked, glancing up from the TV.

"It's my speech," moaned Amanda. "It's *so* bad. The debate is in, like, fifteen hours and I'm *completely* not ready. What am I gonna do?"

"Hold on, hold on," Aunt Livia said comfortingly as she turned off the TV. "It can't be that bad, sweetness. Why don't you practice what you've got so far?"

Amanda shook her head. "It's really bad."

"Oh, I doubt it. Sometimes the hardest part is the first time you say it out loud. Go on! You can trust us. And we'll be able to help out if you need it—give you feedback and comments."

As Amanda took a deep breath and looked down at her notes, no one noticed Matthew slip into the kitchen.

"That was great!" Aunt Livia said when Amanda finished. "I love the part where you tie your food experience into the changes you'd make in the cafeteria."

"Yeah," agreed Molly.

"I did think your delivery was a little rushed," Aunt Livia said thoughtfully. "I know you're nervous, but try to pace yourself. Don't forget to breathe."

Amanda nodded. "That's what Elizabeth said—no matter how slow you think you're going, you'll probably still speed up when you're nervous."

"Speak slowly and clearly. And try to make eye contact with different people in the audience," Aunt Livia advised.

"Remember, Manda, I'm going to sit right in the front row," said Molly. "So you can just look right down at me if you get scared."

"Thanks," Amanda said gratefully. "The thing is—this feels different from the plays. I don't know why. Maybe because when I'm in a play, I'm, like, someone else, you know? But for the debate, I'll just be myself—up there in front of everyone."

"I understand, honey," Aunt Livia said sympathetically. "But remember what I said to you before? If you act confident, everyone will believe that you really are!"

The twins laughed. "That's a good—"

Whhhhhiiiiirrrrrr!

"*Aaarrrggghhh!*" Matthew yelled from the kitchen.

A look of panic crossed Aunt Livia's face. She jumped up from the couch and ran to the kitchen, with the twins following right behind her. The three stopped short in the doorway, then burst out laughing.

Matthew was standing at the counter, in front of his Barf-o Blender, with chocolate ice cream and milk dripping from his face, his hair, the wall, even the ceiling. He looked completely stunned!

"Oh, Matthew! Oh, sweetie! What happened?" gasped Aunt Livia as she tried to catch her breath from laughing. "Did you want a milkshake?"

Matthew nodded numbly. "I was making a milkshake for Amanda," he explained, wiping ice cream out of his eyes. "Mom always makes me one when I feel bad. So I thought maybe Amanda needed one. But—it just went everywhere. I don't know why."

"Matthew! That's the sweetest thing ever!" Amanda exclaimed, swooping down and giving her brother a big, slobbery kiss on the cheek.

"*Eww!*" he complained, wiping his face on his sleeve—and smearing ice cream on his shirt.

"*Mmm.* Delicious," Amanda said, smacking her lips.

"Did you leave the top off the blender?" Aunt Livia asked kindly. "That would do it."

"Yeah, I guess so," Matthew admitted. "I'm sorry. It made a really big mess." A glob of ice cream fell off the ceiling and plopped on his head, making everyone crack up again.

"No worries," Aunt Livia said cheerfully. "Now, here's the plan. I think we could all use a milkshake tonight. So I'll clean up the kitchen. Molly and Amanda, would you get Matthew cleaned up and ready for bed? Then let's all meet up back here in, say, twenty minutes, and Matthew and I will dazzle you girls with the best milkshakes you've ever tasted."

"Awesome!" Matthew cheered, bounding up the stairs, his sisters following behind him.

"Oh, Amanda," Aunt Livia called as Amanda was about to leave the kitchen. "After Matthew goes to bed, you can stay up a little later and we'll go over your speech a few more times. By the time you give it tomorrow at school, you'll be able to do it in your sleep!"

"Thanks, Aunt Livia," Amanda said gratefully, and hurried upstairs to the bathroom where Molly was getting a bath ready for Matthew. *I wish Aunt Livia lived a little closer*, Amanda thought wistfully. *She's so fun and cool and...real.*

The next morning, Amanda woke as the first gray light of dawn peeked around the window shade. Her heart started pounding before she even realized what day it was—the day of the debate.

"Ohhhh," she moaned, rolling over and pulling her

pillow over her head. Across the room, Molly stirred, still asleep.

Amanda glanced at the alarm clock, which was set to go off in less than forty minutes. *There's no point to going back to sleep now,* she thought. *As if I could fall asleep again when I feel this stressed out.* With a sigh, Amanda slipped out of bed and softly padded downstairs.

Aunt Livia was already up, sipping a steaming mug of coffee at the kitchen table and reading *the New York Times.* "You're up early, sweetness," she said as Amanda slumped into the room and sat down next to her at the table. "Can I make you some breakfast? A bagel? Oatmeal? There's time for pancakes if you want them."

Amanda shook her head. "No way! I already feel like I'm gonna throw up," she said, making a face.

Aunt Livia nodded wisely. "That's nerves, honey. But you've got to eat something before school. You don't want to pass out onstage when you give your big speech! Kidding, kidding," she said quickly when she saw Amanda's look of alarm. But it was enough to convince Amanda to choke down some toast and applesauce before going back upstairs to get dressed.

Molly was awake, pulling on her blue-and-white striped sweater over her favorite jeans. "Good morning!" she said brightly. "Are you ready?"

Amanda stood at the closet, where her outfit—a lacy lilac top over a black flare skirt and her cool boots—was ready to go. She paused for a moment. "I don't *feel* ready," she admitted. "But I guess I'm as ready as I'm gonna be. I just wish I didn't feel so much dread about the whole thing! What if everyone laughs at me? What if I sound like a moron? What if I blank out?"

"You won't," Molly said confidently. "A two-minute speech? That's going to be a piece of cake for you!"

Amanda smiled weakly. *I wish I felt as good about this as everyone else does.*

The more Amanda worried about the assembly, the faster the morning slipped by. At 10:45, she joined the rest of the candidates in the empty auditorium with Mr. Degregorio. Mr. D.'s voice echoed in the huge room as he gave the candidates one last pep talk.

"I know you're all going to be fantastic," he said cheerfully. "Now, one last review of the rules: No direct attacks on your opponents. No speeches longer than three minutes. No promises you know you can't keep." Mr. D. glanced at his watch. "The other students should be coming in soon, so let's get backstage."

Behind the heavy, red velvet curtains, two spotlights cast pools of light on the gleaming wooden stage. Amanda took a deep breath as she heard the auditorium

doors bang open and the noisy yells and laughter of students filing into the auditorium. She pictured Molly and the Chef Girls sitting in the front row, and felt a little calmer.

Omar stood next to her. "Hey, Amanda, how you doin'?" he asked quietly.

She shrugged. "I'm kind of nervous."

Omar nodded. "Me, too," he said seriously. "But it's cool! You'll be fine."

Amanda smiled. "I just hope no one laughs at me."

"Really? 'Cause I hope they do. Laugh at me, I mean." Omar waggled his eyebrows up and down, which made Amanda giggle. A few feet away, she noticed Angie standing in stony silence, pretending that Amanda and Omar weren't right there, weren't having fun, weren't leaving her out.

Amanda felt a brief burst of pity for Angie, who always seemed to be separate from other kids—even when she was in the middle of a group. *Oh well, it's her own fault for being so mean*, Amanda thought.

Suddenly, with a loud *whoosh*, the red curtain opened and the stage was flooded with light. From the wings, Amanda saw that every seat in the darkened auditorium was filled—there were far more people there than ever came to the school plays. Just as she was about to panic, though, Omar glanced over at her and made that funny face again. Amanda couldn't help but smile back.

Mr. Degregorio walked out to the front of the stage and stood at one of the podiums.

"Welcome, ladies and gentlemen, to the class president debates! Over the next few minutes, we'll hear from each of the candidates. Let's begin with the eighth-grade candidates—Evan Anderson and Anisha Bhat."

Amanda watched as Evan and Anisha walked onto the stage and took their places at two of the podiums. When Evan spoke, he was calm and sure of himself. *You can feel how the kids out there like him,* she thought. *They're really into what he's talking about.*

All too soon, Anisha's speech was over, and it was time for the seventh-grade candidates. Amanda felt her heart pounding in her ears as she walked onto the bright stage and the audience applauded politely. *I don't wanna go first I don't wanna go first,* she thought. As she looked out into the auditorium, Amanda spotted Molly sitting in the front row. Molly grinned up at her and gave her the thumbs-up sign. Amanda tried to smile back.

Then there was quiet in the massive auditorium—quiet except for kids shuffling in their seats, coughing, clearing their throats—and Amanda knew it was time to begin.

Breathe, she told herself.

"Good-morning!-I'm-Amanda-Moore-and-I'm-running-for-seventh-grade-class-president."

Slow down.

"I love Windsor Middle School, and I have a lot of ideas

for ways the seventh-grade class can make it even better—for us and for everyone else."

You're doing this—and it's good!

"Who here eats the school lunch? Wait—who here *likes* the school lunch?" Amanda paused as some kids in the audience chuckled—it was obvious that they *didn't* like school lunch at all! "Let's face it—it's gross," she continued, pausing again as more kids joined in the laughter. "But it doesn't have to be! For a year and a half now, I've had a cooking business with my sister and our best friends. And we've learned a lot about good food and how to make it. If I'm elected, I will share what I know with the cafeteria ladies. No more greasy pizza, no more soggy canned peas, no more slimy sloppy joes!"

Amanda paused as the kids in the audience cheered and a few applauded.

"Everybody always hears about school budget problems, right? Well, I think that we kids can do some-thing about it. I want the seventh-grade class to work together to put on the biggest fundraiser this school has ever seen! A carnival that the entire neighborhood could enjoy—and could help us raise the money we need for better field trips and more activities. And maybe even a big dance for all of us at the end of the year! This fall, I helped the Windsor Volunteers' Club with a charity harvest fundraiser. I know what to do and how to do it. And I know that everybody at this school deserves Moore.

Moore food, Moore fun, Moore for president! Thank you very much."

Amanda looked out in the auditorium, where kids had started clapping loudly and whistling. *They liked my speech!* she thought in a daze. *They liked me!*

Beside her, Angie cleared her throat impatiently. *It's driving her crazy that people are clapping for me,* Amanda thought. Remembering that she was still onstage, Amanda resisted the urge to roll her eyes.

When the applause died down, Angie began to speak. "Hey, everybody! My name is Angie Martinez—but you all knew that already. And I'm running for seventh-grade class prez. I think the school lunches are bad, too—but I actually have a way to fix them that'll work. We need to have vending machines installed in the cafeteria—not just by the gym. Then everybody could pick what they want. Because lunch should be about having choices, you know?"

Yeah, the choice of junk food, Amanda thought angrily. *Great solution, Angie! Not!*

"And I also want more cool assemblies. Sometimes the assemblies are pretty boring, but even so, there aren't enough of them. I think that assemblies are a good way to learn stuff outside of class. But they should be cooler. So that's another thing I would change.

"Oh, yeah—I can't believe I forgot! I want Windsor to have music at lunch. So, like, every day, you could go to lunch and request a song, and it would be played in the caf.

Like radio but, um, just in our caf. Because Windsor *rocks*! Right? Say it with me! Windsor *rocks*! *Woo-hoo!*" Angie stepped in front of the podium and did a split. The crowd cheered.

Amanda felt a flash of anger. *She is such a show-off!* But then it was Omar's turn, and Angie was forgotten for the moment.

Omar pulled the microphone out of its holder and walked in front of the podium. He did a funny dance step and then started rapping!

"You know I'm the man
Omar Kazdan!
And I got a plan
Omar Kazdan!
To rock WMS!
Omar Kazdan!
Like only I can!
Omar Kazdan!
When you look around, whatcha see is whatcha get.
But with me around, I'm gonna change all of that!
Study hall, what is that, it's just a big waste.
Sittin' in a chair in the same old place?
Me, I say no way, that's a waste of my time.
Get your stuff together now and listen to my rhyme:
Music room, computer room, library, too—
You can learn just as well doin' what you wanna do!

So I say: Passes get you where you wanna be.
Learnin' what you wanna learn and doin' it for free!"

Two boys in the audience—Amanda suspected it was Justin and Connor—stood up and started calling, "*Omar! Omar! Omar!*" Soon, the rest of the audience had joined in, and kids clapped along to the beat.

"Now I got one more thing that I wanna say.
My fav'rite food is pizza; I could eat it every day.
And if you vote me prez, that's what we're gonna do.
Cuz Pizza Roma makes the best,
and they'll deliver here to school!"

As Omar finished rapping, the audience erupted into loud cheers and laughter. Even the teachers were smiling as Mr. Degregorio quickly walked onstage, holding up his hands to quiet down the rowdy students.

Amanda hurried off the stage as the candidates for sixth-grade class president took their places at the podiums. Her face was splotchy and red. *How did that happen? How did Omar steal the show like that?* she wondered. *If the election was tomorrow, he would totally win. My speech was so lame compared to his.*

Lost in her own thoughts, Amanda didn't notice when someone came up behind her and tapped her shoulder.

"Huh? What?" she asked, spinning around. "Oh, hi, Evan!"

"Hey—good speech, Amanda."

Amanda rolled her eyes. "I don't know. Last night I thought it was good, but now it seems pretty lame."

Evan shook his head. "No, you were really sincere. You've got some great ideas. I would vote for you if I was still in seventh grade. Anyone who knows how to clean up the cafeteria food deserves to be president!"

Amanda smiled at him. "Thanks. Your speech was great, too."

Evan shrugged. "Same old, same old. I don't even get nervous anymore. This is the third time I've run for class president! Hey, I was wondering something...are you busy Friday night? 'Cause it's the first basketball game of the season here at Windsor and, uh, I was wondering if you want to go?"

Amanda blinked. *Is...does he mean...like a date?* She swallowed. "Oh, yeah. I love the basketball games. They're really fun."

"Great! The game starts at six, so I'll pick you up around five-thirty. Does that sound okay?"

Amanda nodded, hardly believing her ears. *It is a date! Ohmigosh!*

"All right! See ya!" Evan flashed Amanda a smile and, with a little wave, walked out of the auditorium into the hall.

Evan Anderson asked me out on a date!

Evan Anderson...likes me!

103

chapter 10

"*A*unt Livia! Aunt Livia!"

"Amanda! How was it?"

"It was *amazing*! The kids seemed to really like my ideas. And I stayed calm and remembered to breathe, just like you told me. Everybody laughed—in a good way!— when I talked about how gross school lunch is."

Aunt Livia gave Amanda a big hug. "I knew you'd be terrific!"

"Thanks! Of course Angie's speech was totally boring and predictable, but she finished it with splits—she thinks she's such a big shot. Omar really blew everybody away, though—he did a rap!"

"Really?" Aunt Livia laughed. "That must have been crazy."

"It was," Molly spoke up. "Omar's nuts."

"It worked, though—everyone was screaming and cheering. I kinda wish I'd done something different," Amanda said. Then she shrugged. "Oh well. My speech went really well, and it's over now, and that's all that matters. Oh, but guess what else!"

"What?"

"Evan Anderson asked me out *on a date*!"

Aunt Livia's eyes grew wide and her mouth dropped open. "My goodness! Come into the kitchen—I made some apple spice cake—and tell me all about it! And I want to hear more about the debate, too."

As she hung up her coat, Molly rolled her eyes. Amanda had been talking about Evan Anderson all day long, and she didn't seem ready to stop yet. Molly joined Amanda and Aunt Livia in the kitchen, cutting herself a piece of the warm cake before sitting at the table.

"And it's *this Friday night*! I can't *even* believe it! What do you think I should wear? On my first date ever?"

Aunt Livia raised her eyebrows. "Hold on a minute, Manda. Would your mom let you go on a date?"

I don't think so, Molly thought to herself.

Amanda stopped. She hadn't thought of that. "Of course!" she heard herself say. "She lets us hang out with guys all the time. Justin, Connor, Omar. Molly and Justin spent, like, every minute together on the Cape last summer."

Molly shot her sister "the look." This time, it meant, *You* know *that's not the same thing.*

But nobody noticed it.

Thursday morning, Amanda and Molly picked up Shawn on the way to school.

"Hey, girl!" Shawn grinned at Amanda. "So what's next on the campaign front?"

"Well, we still have to do the cookie bake-off the day before the election. And the big party this Saturday night! Oh, and Natasha's going to write that article about me for *the Post.*"

Molly shook her head. "Didn't she tell you? Ms. Zane said that she would have to interview the other candidates, too—and Natasha really doesn't want to interview Angie."

"Oh," Amanda sounded surprised. "No, she didn't mention anything. That's weird." The three girls walked in silence for a few moments until they reached the school. "Oh, I need some advice!" Amanda exclaimed. "If my *date* goes well on Friday night, do you think I should invite Evan to our party? Or is that weird? Maybe I should just wait until he asks me to do something else. Or maybe—what is it, Shawn?"

Shawn had stopped short, a look of shock on her face. She shook her head and pointed to the wall in front of them, where her biggest, best poster had hung.

Now it was in shreds. Brightly colored scraps were scattered through the hall.

"*Ohmigosh,*" the twins breathed at the same time, too horrified to say any more. Amanda turned to Shawn and Molly with outrage in her eyes.

"My poster! How—Who—How did this happen?" she cried. Amanda spun on her heel and raced down the hall, with Molly and Shawn following her. Then Amanda stopped so suddenly that Molly almost ran into her.

On the floor in front of them, another two posters lay in shreds.

Tears of anger and hurt welled up in Amanda's eyes. "Oh, Shawn, all of your hard work! Who would do this?"

Shawn only shook her head, staring silently at the destroyed posters. Sighing heavily, she bent down and began to pick up the pieces.

"Well, I know who did it," Amanda went on. "Angie. She is so evil! She's the worst person I've ever known! She's been out to get me since last year. I don't know *why* she is always picking on me, but it's *not* going to go on any longer! I've had it with her!"

"Manda." Shawn's voice was quiet, but there was an edge of tension in it—like what she was about to say was painful for her. "Manda. I think—I think she did this to get me, too."

Amanda and Shawn looked at each other for a long moment. Then Amanda reached down and snatched the poster pieces from Shawn's hands. "Well, I've had enough. She is *not* going to get away with this!"

As Amanda stormed off down the hall, Molly put her hand on Shawn's arm. "Shawn, I'm so sorry," she said quietly. "I know how hard you worked on those posters. They were so beautiful."

Shawn smiled sadly at Molly. "Thanks, Molls. I feel

kind of—I don't even know. It's so awful to see them torn to pieces like that. I did work really, really hard. I was—I was really proud of them." She looked down quickly, and Molly could tell she was trying not to cry.

Moments later, Amanda rushed into Mr. Degregorio's classroom. Homeroom was about to start, and he looked up from his desk, surprised to see her.

"Amanda, social studies is next period," he started to joke, then stopped abruptly when he saw her face. "What's wrong?"

Amanda dropped the pieces of her ruined posters on his desk. "Someone destroyed my posters!" she cried, feeling tears prick at her eyes. "And I know who did it!"

Mr. D. looked down and sighed heavily. "Let's talk in the hallway," he said softly, putting his hand on Amanda's elbow and leading her out of the classroom, where all of the students had been watching them intently.

Once they were in the hall, Mr. D. closed the door behind them. "Amanda, I'm so sorry this happened to you. Unfortunately, politics can be dirty. But it shouldn't be at this level. I am extremely upset."

"It was Angie Martinez!" Amanda said between her teeth.

"Did you see her rip up your posters?" Mr. Degregorio asked in a serious tone.

Amanda looked down at the ground. "Well, no. I didn't actually *see* her do it. But I *know* it was her. She's hated me since last year. And she hates my best friend, Shawn, who decided to help with my campaign instead of hers. Besides, no one else would do this! I just *know* it was Angie."

Mr. D. shook his head. "I'm sorry, Amanda. But unless there's an eyewitness who saw Angie—or anyone else—rip down your posters, there's nothing we can do. However, I'll have a serious talk with each candidate about playing fair." He smiled gently. "I know how angry you are, and you have every right to be. But try to stay focused on the positive—you're running a great campaign, and you don't have any need to ruin someone else's property to make yourself feel better. Okay?"

Amanda nodded sadly. In her mind, she knew Mr. D. was right—there wasn't anything he could do without proof. But in her heart, she was sure it was Angie.

"I'll write you a pass to homeroom," Mr. Degregorio said. "And I'll see you in a few minutes for class."

"Thanks, Mr. D."

When Amanda walked into homeroom a few minutes later, Molly was anxiously watching her. Amanda smiled weakly at her twin to let her know she was doing okay. Then her eyes fell on Angie, who was also watching her. Angie's eyes burned with a hard, bright happiness, and her lips curled into an ugly sneer as she saw how upset Amanda was.

At that instant, Amanda *knew*, without a doubt, that Angie was the one who had destroyed her posters.

You are not *going to get away with this, Angie,* Amanda thought with growing determination. *Not this time.*

After school, Molly had a meeting for *the Post*, but Amanda went straight home. She had a plan to get even with Angie and she wanted to start right away. Grabbing an apple from the kitchen, she hurried into the den and turned on the computer. Then she went upstairs to her room and found last year's yearbook. Angie's picture was on page sixty-seven. *By tomorrow, everyone will know all about you, Angie,* Amanda thought.

Amanda scanned Angie's picture into the computer, then dropped it into a Word document. She typed quickly, and a few minutes later, she hit the Print icon and looked at the flyer she'd made.

Perfect, Amanda thought. She printed thirty copies. *Now you'll see how it feels, Angie.*

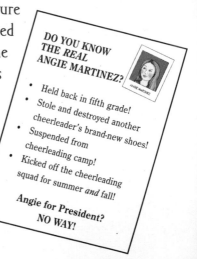

DO YOU KNOW THE REAL ANGIE MARTINEZ?

- Held back in fifth grade!
- Stole and destroyed another cheerleader's brand-new shoes!
- Suspended from cheerleading camp!
- Kicked off the cheerleading squad for summer *and* fall!

Angie for President? NO WAY!

When Molly got home from the meeting half an hour later, Amanda was waiting for her.

"Check it out," Amanda said, handing Molly one of the flyers before she had even taken off her coat. "I can play dirty, too."

Molly read over the flyer quickly, then sighed as she handed it back to Amanda. "This is a *really* bad idea, Manda," she said bluntly. "Really bad. Besides, why do you want to be evil like Angie, anyway?"

Amanda stepped back, stunned by her twin's reaction. "Molly! What are you talking about? I'm sick of letting Angie walk all over me. I'm just standing up for myself."

Molly rolled her eyes. "Don't do it, Amanda. It's gonna backfire." She shook her head and lugged her heavy backpack upstairs to start her homework, leaving Amanda standing alone in the hall.

All at once, Amanda felt embarrassed and angry. *Who cares what Molly thinks?* she thought. *I don't need her help. Or Natasha's. Or anybody's! This is my campaign and I'll do what I want!*

The next morning, as the Moores were eating break-fast, the doorbell rang. Aunt Livia raised her eyebrows at the twins, then went to answer the door. Molly and Amanda exchanged glances as they wondered, *Who's that?*

It was Natasha.

"Um, Natasha, what's up?" Molly asked.

"Would you like some juice or toast?" Aunt Livia asked.

Natasha shook her head. "No thanks, I already ate," she answered. "Um, sorry for dropping by like this. I, uh, wanted to talk to Amanda before school."

Amanda swallowed her mouthful of oatmeal. "Sure."

Natasha looked down for a moment. "Um...I can't write an article about you for *the Post.* Ms. Zane says if I write about you, I have to write about Omar and Angie, too. Omar would be fine, but...I'm really sorry, Amanda. I just can't interview Angie. I really don't like her, and—and I'm kind of scared of her, too. I hope you're not mad."

Amanda smiled at Natasha. "I'm not mad. It's okay," she said—and she meant it.

Natasha smiled gratefully. "Thanks for understanding! Anyway, I've been thinking about some other way to help with your campaign. And then, last night, I realized that I could make up that flyer for you. Remember the one we talked about? Well, anyway, here it is. I hope you like it."

Silently, Amanda read the flyer, with Molly looking

over her shoulder. "*Ohmigosh*, Natasha! This is wonderful! I can't believe you did this for me. That's so sweet."

"My dad took me to the copy shop last night and I had them printed in a bunch of different colors," Natasha said, smiling as she pulled out stacks of pink, blue, green, and lavender paper from her backpack. "I'm so glad you like it!"

"It's perfect," Amanda said. "Um, I'll be right back. Thank you *so* much, Natasha!"

Amanda hurried upstairs to her room and closed the door behind her. She opened her backpack and took out the stack of nasty flyers she had made about Angie. *While Natasha was making me that great flyer yesterday, I was busy making this horrible one about Angie.* Amanda shivered as she realized how close she'd been to spreading those flyers all over school—and acting just as evil as Angie.

No, Amanda thought firmly. *Just because Angie is awful doesn't mean I have to be.*

She ripped the flyers in half and threw them in the trash. *Today is a new day*, she told herself, running back downstairs.

113

Amanda had better things to think about than
Angie, anyway. It was Friday—and her date with Evan was
just a few hours away! *I wonder if he'll bring me
flowers,* she thought dreamily. *I wonder if he'll hold my
hand!* As excited as Amanda felt, though, she couldn't
quite shake a nagging feeling that maybe, if Mom were
home, she wouldn't allow Amanda to go on a real date.

No, Mom would understand, she tried to reassure
herself. *I think...*

At lunchtime, Amanda noticed several kids around her

wearing large blue buttons on their shirts and
pinning them onto their backpacks. Amanda
took a closer look, and saw that the buttons had
a big picture of Omar smiling his goofy grin,
with the words "KAZDAN—DA MAN!" on them. In the
middle of a crowd stood Omar, clowning around as usual.
"Ladies and gentlemen, step right up!" he called out, like
a barker at a carnival. "Come and see the eighth wonder
of the world—the one, the only, *me*—Omar Kazdan, your
next president. That's right, Kazdan, Da Man."

*Buttons—what a great idea. Why didn't I think of
that?* Amanda thought, shaking her head. *Oh, well. I've*

got my cookie bake-off. People would rather eat my homemade cookies than wear a button with Omar's face on it any day—I hope.

On the walk home from school that afternoon, Amanda was practically skipping with excitement. Molly couldn't help but smile at how happy her sister was, though in her heart she wished Amanda would just hang out with the girls that night.

"Molls, what do you think I should wear?" Amanda asked, biting her lip in concentration. "This is tough—I can't be *too* dressed up, 'cause it's just a basketball game. But I still want to look good, you know?"

Molly shrugged. "What's wrong with what you're wearing now?" she asked.

Amanda looked down at her flared jeans and gray-and-blue sweater. "No way!" she replied, shaking her head. "Way too...blah." She sighed dramatically. "Oh well, I *guess* I'll figure something out!"

Despite Amanda's worries, she had no trouble getting ready, even though she had to call Shawn three times to ask her opinion about which outfit to wear. Finally, Amanda decided on black corduroy pants with a silver and green top with bell sleeves, and sparkly silver earrings.

Around five o'clock, Aunt Livia popped her head in,

with Matthew right behind her. "How's it going?" she asked, her eyes twinkling. "Any fashion catastrophes?"

"Nope," replied Molly without looking up from the magazine she was reading. "Not a one."

"Molly, sweetie, are you going to the game?" Aunt Livia asked, noticing that Molly was lounging around in her sweatpants.

Molly shook her head. "Uh-uh. I don't really feel like it. I'd rather stay home and chill." Molly glanced down at her magazine before Aunt Livia could look in her eyes and see the truth—that Molly didn't want to be in the way on her sister's first date.

"Oh, Aunt Livia, can you help me with something *very* important?" Amanda, who hadn't heard Molly, asked from the bathroom, where she was applying lip gloss. "I got this really pretty green eye shadow...can you show me how to put it on?"

Aunt Livia raised her eyebrows as she walked over to the bathroom. "Actually, Amanda, the way it works is that when you're old enough to wear eye shadow, you automatically know how to put it on."

Amanda stared at her aunt. "Are you for real?"

Aunt Livia burst out laughing. "That's what Nana always told your mom and me. It actually kept us from wearing eye shadow until college! But I think I can help you out. Let's see..." Aunt Livia gently swept the applicator over Amanda's eyelids. "What do you think?"

Amanda opened her eyes and admired the shimmery pale green shadow that brought out the emerald in her eyes. "Thanks *so* much!" she squealed. "It looks awesome! So sophisticated!"

"*Soooo sophisticated!*" Matthew mimicked his sister in a high-pitched voice. "I look *soooo* beautiful. Oh, *Evan! Mwa! Mwa! Mwa! Mwa-arghhh!*"

Amanda tossed a pillow at her brother, stopping him from making fun of her—for a moment, at least. "Don't be a pain, Matthew!" she warned him.

Just then, the doorbell rang. "Oh, *no!*" Amanda cried. "He's early! Help! I still have to put on my shoes—oh, no, Aunt Livia! *Please* don't let Matthew answer the door! *Please!*"

But it was too late—Matthew was already racing down the stairs.

"Amanda, finish getting ready. I'll do damage control downstairs," Aunt Livia said as she hurried out of the twins' room. Then she poked her head back in. "Have a blast tonight!"

As Amanda pulled on her shoes, she heard Aunt Livia greeting Evan at the door, then Matthew saying, "You like my sister? Really? Why?" before Aunt Livia ordered him to wait in the kitchen. Amanda sighed with relief as she heard Matthew, who was still giggling, obey. *I am definitely gonna get him later!* she thought.

With a deep breath, Amanda stood up and took one

more look in the mirror, fluffing her hair and straightening her top.

"You look great, Amanda," Molly's voice cut through her thoughts.

"Oh, thanks!" Amanda said. For a moment, she had forgotten Molly was still in the room with her.

The worst part was that Molly could tell.

"Well, have fun," Molly said awkwardly.

Amanda grinned. "I will! Oh, wow, I'm so nervous! Ack!" She grabbed her small black purse off the desk and hurried out the door. "Bye! See you tonight!"

Molly listened to Amanda and Evan greet each other, then heard the door slam behind them. She could still smell Amanda's perfume. Amanda and Molly always hung out together on Friday nights—sometimes with their friends, sometimes with their family, sometimes with just each other. *But I guess that's over,* Molly thought sadly. *Now Amanda's gonna be going out with boys, having a great time...* Even though Amanda would be back in a few hours, Molly suddenly missed her sister terribly.

A light rain began falling as Evan and Amanda walked to Windsor Middle School. Fortunately, Evan had brought an umbrella.

"That was a good idea," Amanda said, shivering in the chilly air.

"Yeah, my dad thought of it," Evan replied.

"Oh, good." There was a pause as Amanda racked her brain frantically, trying to think of something—anything—to say. "Um, how's school?" she finally asked.

"Pretty good. I have a lot more homework this year than last year, though. So that's not great."

"Oh, no, don't tell me that!" joked Amanda. "Is *that* what I have to look forward to?"

Evan nodded seriously. "Oh, yeah. *Tons* of home-work." A grin spread across his face and Amanda could tell he was kidding.

"Quit messing with me!" she cried, pretending to be upset. "You eighth-graders are always picking on us poor seventh-graders!"

"Hey, if you can't take the heat..." Evan joked back.

When they arrived at the gym, Evan reached in front of Amanda to open the door for her.

"Thanks," Amanda said, thinking, *Wow! He's so polite!*

Amanda followed Evan up the bleachers to a bench in the middle of the stands. Amanda looked around the gym, seeing kids she knew from her classes. *I wonder if they can tell we're together, on a date,* she thought. *Oh, boy—I'm not sure what to say next. Why is Evan so quiet? And why does he keep tapping his fingers on the bench? That's kind of annoying.*

Oblivious, Evan kept drumming his fingers and glancing around the gym. *Is he bored?* Amanda fretted. *Yipes! I've got to think of* something *to say!*

Then she noticed Justin and Omar a few rows away, glancing up at her. "Miss Amanda Moore!" Omar called out. "What's up? Where's your double?"

"Oh, um, Molly's at home," Amanda answered.

Omar raised his eyebrows. "Never thought I'd see that happen," he joked. "Who are you here with? Is that wacky Peichi around?"

Amanda froze. *Ack, this is weird!* she thought suddenly, feeling strangely embarrassed to tell Omar and Justin she was on a date. "Um, I'm, I'm here with, um, Evan." She turned to Evan, hoping he wouldn't notice her blushing. "Evan, do you know Omar Kazdan and Justin McElroy?"

"What's up," Evan said.

Justin just nodded and looked out toward the gym floor.

"Omar, nice buttons. I've seen tons of kids wearing them today," Evan continued.

"Thanks, man," Omar replied. "You want one?"

Justin leaned over to Omar to say something, and once again, Amanda was left with Evan—with nothing to say to him.

"Your campaign seems really good," she finally blurted out.

Evan smiled, looking relieved that she'd said something.

"Yeah," he said modestly. "I think it's going well. You never know what will happen on election day, though. So I'm trying not to get too confident or anything."

Amanda nodded. "That's a good way to look at it," she agreed. As she paused to think of something else to say, Evan started drumming on the bench again. Suddenly Amanda realized, *Evan's nervous, too! He's having trouble thinking of what to say! He's not bored or too cool for me. He's just nervous. Whew!*

"Oh, here come the cheerleaders!" Amanda exclaimed as the gym doors burst open and the squad ran onto the floor. "My best friend Shawn—she's in the front there—she was just promoted to center front. She's awesome!" Shawn saw Amanda then, and gave her a little wave. Amanda waved back—and noticed Angie standing behind Shawn, staring up at Amanda and Evan.

"Hi, Evan!" Angie sang out from the gym floor, waving.

Amanda felt like her heart skipped a beat. *Oh, no,* she thought. *No way. When did they let Angie back on the squad?*

Angie started climbing the bleachers, heading right for them.

Please don't ruin this, Angie, Amanda thought desperately. *Please go away. Oh, I wish Molly was here. She always stays cool when things go wrong.*

Of course, Angie sat right down on Evan's other side.

"Oh, hi, Angie," Evan said. "What's up?"

"Not much," Angie replied cheerfully. "Just getting ready for the opening routine. We're doing some really awesome cheers this winter. I can't wait to hear what you think!"

"Angie, you know Amanda, right?" Evan asked, turning to Amanda.

Angie rolled her eyes. "Uh, yeah. But Evan, I have to ask you a *very* important question—*what* are you doing after the game?"

"Well, actually—" Evan began.

"Because *I'm* going to Pizza Roma, and you should totally come! It's gonna be way fun. Paul is going, and so is Ashley. What do you say? *Please*!"

Amanda sat there, dumbfounded, as Angie tried to steal her date away.

Evan turned to Amanda awkwardly. "Um, do you—"

Just then, Coach Carson barked, "Angie!"

Angie widened her eyes. "*Ooh*, I'm so busted!" she giggled. "See you after the game, E.!" She bounded down the bleachers, her long blonde ponytail bouncing behind her.

Amanda's heart sank as she thought, *Angie's going to ruin my first date ever.* She imagined herself in a booth with Evan and Angie, who would act like Amanda wasn't even there.

"Amanda?" Evan asked, breaking into her thoughts. "Uh, do you want to go to Pizza Roma after the game? 'Cause I had pizza for lunch and I don't really want it again. I was thinking maybe we could go somewhere else. If you want to."

"Absolutely!" Amanda exclaimed happily, trying not to sound *too* relieved. "I know this really cool place called Harry's. They have the best desserts. And really good wraps, too."

"Cool," Evan said, smiling.

Amanda noticed he wasn't tapping his fingers anymore. She smiled back at Evan, then looked out at the gym floor, where she noticed Angie watching them with a worried expression. *Sorry, Angie,* Amanda thought briefly, *but you're not going to ruin this for me.*

When Amanda got home that night, Aunt Livia was waiting for her in the living room. "Hi, sweetness! Did you have a good time?" she asked as Amanda came in.

Amanda nodded, grinning. "I had an awesome time! I'll be right back to tell you all about it." She raced up the stairs two at a time to the room she shared with Molly. She flung open the door and squealed, "*Ohmigosh,* Molls, I had the *weirdest* night ever!"

"What happened?"

"Well, it was so *weird* being with Evan on a date! Like, I couldn't think of anything to say. And he kept drumming his fingers on *everything,* which was totally annoying! And we ran into Justin and Omar, which felt really awkward. They were asking where you were and I was thinking, 'Yeah, where is Molly?' 'Cause I missed you! Oh, but then the *worst* happened—Angie tried to butt into *our* date! But Evan was so sweet about it, he ended up blowing her off. So then we went to Harry's and everything was...easier—once we didn't have, like, the entire school watching us, you know? But *ugh*, it still felt totally stressful!" Amanda flopped back on her bed, sighing dramatically, which made Molly smile.

"So, what else?" Molly asked. "Did Evan...did he, um, kiss you?"

Amanda popped back up. "Oh, *no way*! He didn't even hold my hand or anything. And I'm *glad*! It was weird enough trying to think of things to say to each other, you know?"

"Oh. So you don't like him anymore?" Molly asked carefully, trying to figure out what was going on. Amanda was talking so fast it was hard to keep up with her story!

"What? He's so cute and nice and really polite and sweet and, *ohhhh*, Molls, he's so cute! And nice!" Amanda pressed her hand over her heart and sighed again. "I still like him. I just like him better when there are other people around, you know? And seriously, at the game, I kept missing you. It was so strange to be out with Evan without any of my girls around—especially without you."

Molly nodded. She knew exactly what Amanda meant.

"So, what did you do tonight?" Amanda asked.

"Aunt Livia and Matthew and I made cookie dough—
tons of cookie dough! It's all in the freezer, so on
Wednesday, all we have to do is bake the cookies. Then we
can hand 'em out Thursday morning before the
election."

"Molls! Thank you! That's awesome!"
exclaimed Amanda, jumping over to her sister's
bed and giving Molly a big hug.

Molly hugged Amanda back, then asked, "So how was
the game? Who won? And what was the score?"

Amanda looked at her blankly. "Huh? Oh, um,
Windsor won. I don't know what the score was. I wasn't
really paying attention, you know?" Amanda yawned.
"Boy, am I tired. Dating is *exhausting!* Not to mention
we're having our party tomorrow, and I definitely need
some beauty sleep." She went to the bathroom to brush
her teeth.

Molly shook her head, smiling. *That's just like
Amanda*, she thought. *Maybe everything isn't going to
change, after all.*

The next day, Shawn, Peichi, and Natasha arrived to help Molly and Amanda get ready for their party.

"Okay! Molls and I decided to do a pasta bar tonight," Amanda said once everyone was in the kitchen.

"What's that?" Peichi asked.

"I've never heard of a pasta bar, either," Natasha said.

"It's totally cool!" Amanda explained. "Aunt Livia went to a fancy party in Los Angeles that had one. Basically, you cook a bunch of pasta. Then you have different sauces—Molls and I want to serve pesto, marinara, cream sauce, and olive oil. And a bunch of veggies and meats like chicken, meatballs, and sausage. You set up a hot plate, and people come up and pick out their favorite ingredients, and you make up their meal right in front of them!"

"That is such a neat idea!" exclaimed Shawn. "All that stuff is easy to make. But people will be really impressed!"

"I think so, too," Amanda agreed. "And I'll sauté every-body's food, so that way I can tell them to vote for me! And we're gonna make ice-cream sundaes for dessert. We picked out five different kinds of ice cream and a ton of toppings—nuts, cherries, sprinkles, crushed candy bars, whipped cream, *everything*!"

Shawn was right—the food for the pasta bar wasn't hard to make. But it was time-consuming, just because there were so many choices! Peichi cooked three pounds of pasta—penne, linguine, and rotini— while Amanda and Shawn made the sauces. Molly focused on preparing the meats, while Natasha chopped and lightly cooked the vegetables. Before long, it was already after five o'clock—and the party was going to start in less than an hour!

As the girls got ready together in the twins' room, Amanda, as usual, tried to get Molly to dress up.

"No way, Manda. I am *not* wearing a dress," Molly said firmly. "These gray pants are nice—and comfortable, too. And the white sweater is sort of fancy."

"Fine," sighed Amanda. "But your outfit needs...I don't know. Something." She snapped her fingers. "The bracelet! The one with the shells!"

"*Really?*" Molly asked. At the end of the summer, Justin had given Molly a delicate pink shell bracelet. That was how she'd found out that he had a crush on her—and not on Amanda.

"Absolutely," Amanda said. "It pulls the entire outfit together."

After the Chef Girls got ready, they set up the pasta bar in the dining room. At either end of the dining room table was a hot plate on which Molly and Amanda would

sauté each guest's pasta, sauce, and toppings. And in the middle of the table lay pretty bowls of sauces and dish after dish of ingredients—peas, steamed carrots, sliced olives, red and green peppers, broccoli, fresh tomatoes, and some of Molly's own basil.

"It looks fantastic in here!" Aunt Livia exclaimed, poking her head into the dining room as Matthew snuck in to steal an olive. "Even better than the pasta bar at that party I went to."

"I can't wait to eat some of this pasta!" Molly exclaimed. "It's so good to cook with you guys."

"Well, you can always come back to Dish. We do a lot of cooking," Amanda said lightly.

Before Molly could answer, the doorbell rang. The first guest to arrive was Elizabeth.

"Wow, this looks so yummy!" Elizabeth said when she saw the pasta bar. "I'm impressed!"

"Thanks!" Amanda said, smiling. "Would you like something to drink? We have—" Her mind went blank, and then she realized, *Oh, no, we forgot to buy drinks!* "Um, I'll be right back." Amanda hurried to the kitchen where Aunt Livia was loading the dishwasher.

"Aunt Livia! We forgot to buy drinks!" exclaimed Amanda.

A look of surprise crossed Aunt Livia's face. "Darn! I

knew there was something!" She quickly dried her hands on a dishtowel. "I'll go to the store. And I'll take Matthew to keep him out of your hair. Anything in particular you want? Or should I just get a ton of juice and soda?"

"That's fine," Amanda replied. "Thank you!"

Ding-dong!

Connor and Justin arrived next—with Omar!

I cannot even believe that Omar came to my campaign party! Amanda thought, surprised. But she couldn't help smiling as he barreled into the room, then yelled out, "Amanda! Hope you don't mind me crashing the party. But I know what good cooks you Chef Girls are and I couldn't help myself. Man, that looks delicious! If I wasn't running for president, I'd vote for you myself!"

"Ditto," Amanda joked back.

Ding-dong!

"I'll get it," Molly called. When she came back from the door, Justin was waiting in the hallway just outside the dining room.

"Hi, Molly," he said quickly, his face lighting up. "How's everything?"

"Oh, it's good," Molly said, distracted. "I have to—"

"The bracelet looks really good on you," Justin continued. "I haven't seen you wearing it before. I thought maybe you didn't like it."

Shoot! Now he's gonna think I'm, like, madly in love with him, all because I'm wearing this dumb bracelet! Thanks a lot, Manda!

"Oh, I was, um, saving it for a special occasion," she replied. Just then, the doorbell rang again. *Saved by the bell!* "I've gotta get the door. See you in a minute!"

Back in the dining room, Amanda whispered to Shawn, "Everyone we invited is here...should we start the pasta bar now, or wait for Aunt Livia to get back with the drinks?"

Ding-dong!

"Let's wait," Shawn suggested. "You can mingle now and work later."

Ding-dong!

Why does the doorbell keep ringing? Amanda wondered. "I'm going to check in with Molly." In the hall-way, Amanda passed ten or fifteen kids she didn't know. "Um, hi, hi, thanks for coming," she said, pressing past them to get to the door. "Molly! Who are—"

Ding-dong!

"—all these people?" Amanda whispered.

Molly shrugged as she swung open the door. "I thought they were people you knew from campaigning."

Ding-dong!

"This is insane!" Molly continued. "I mean, we should just leave the door open, I guess."

"But we're not gonna have enough food!" Amanda

wailed. "Oh, why isn't Aunt Livia back yet?"

Suddenly, loud rock and roll blasted from Dad's stereo in the living room. The twins exchanged a look and ran to the living room, where people had pushed tables and chairs against the wall to open up a space for dancing.

"Amanda?" Peichi asked from the hall. "Can you come back in the dining room for a minute?"

Amanda followed Peichi to the dining room and gasped when she saw the pasta bar. People were serving themselves, like it was a buffet—and they were almost out of food!

"I'm really sorry!" Peichi said miserably. "They just came in and started *eating*! We didn't know *what* to do! Should I make more pasta?"

Amanda nodded. "I guess so. But we're not gonna have enough!"

Ding-dong!

"Where are all these people coming from?" Amanda exclaimed.

Shawn appeared, looking worried. "Manda, somebody came with this," she said, handing Amanda a folded piece of paper. It was the twins' e-vite—and it had been forwarded to dozens of people!

"*Ohmigosh,*" Amanda breathed. "There's, like, a hundred e-mail addresses on this!"

Crash!

Amanda raced to the living room, where she found

Molly picking up pieces of glass from a broken picture frame. "Molls!" she hissed. "This party is a *disaster*! What are we gonna do?"

"I have no idea! Hopefully, Aunt Livia will be back any minute. She'll know how to take care of it."

"Okay, we're officially out of food," Natasha reported, joining the twins. "I put out some crackers and chips I found in the kitchen, but they're gone, too."

Ding-dong!

Amanda put her head in her hands for a moment, then hurried to the door. It was the delivery guy from Pizza Roma—and he was carrying ten extra-large pizzas!

"What—who ordered pizza?" she asked, surprised.

"Awesome!" cheered an eighth-grade guy behind Amanda. He brushed past her to grab the pizzas. "Pizza's here!" he yelled out to the party, and a swarm of laughing, shrieking kids followed him into the dining room.

"That'll be a hundred and twenty-eight dollars," the pizza guy said.

Amanda's mouth dropped open. "Um, hang on just a minute," she said. She rushed off to the living room, where Molly was trying to turn the volume down on the stereo—again. "Molly!" she cried. "There's a pizza guy here and he wants a hundred and twenty-eight dollars!"

"I'll take care of this one," said Omar, who had overheard her. Amanda and Molly watched as Omar zoomed through

the crowd, calling, "Pizza donations! You eat it, you buy it! Come on, everybody, chip in!"

"We've got to get these people out of here," Molly said. "This is a wreck!"

"But how?" asked Amanda. "We can't just say, 'Everybody go home.' That would be *so* lame!"

"Well, do you have a better idea?" snapped Molly.

Ding-dong!

"*What* is going on here?"

The twins looked up to see Aunt Livia standing in the doorway, a look of shock and horror on her face. "I thought you were having over a *few* friends, not the entire school!"

"So did we, Aunt Livia," Amanda said quickly. "But our e-vite got forwarded all over the place! We don't even *know* half of these people!"

Aunt Livia nodded. "Sorry, girls," she said. Then she charged over to the stereo, unplugged it, and yelled in a firm voice, "Okay, everyone, party over! You don't have to go home, but you can't stay here!"

The kids snickered and rolled their eyes, but to Amanda's relief, they did begin to trickle out. *Everyone's gonna think I'm a huge geek because my party was called off!* she fretted. *Oh, well. Nothing I can do about it now.* She followed Aunt Livia into the dining room, where she made the same announcement.

Omar came up to her then. "Hey, Amanda. I got eighty-four dollars here. Now what are we gonna do about the rest?"

Aunt Livia, who amazingly seemed to be everywhere at once, appeared with her wallet. "I'll pay for the rest," she said.

"Omar, thanks for collecting the pizza money," Amanda said gratefully.

"No problemo," Omar replied. "Thanks for having such a kickin' party. I'm gonna jet, though, before your aunt kicks me out personally. Connor, Justin—wanna go to the arcade?"

Within ten minutes, only the Chef Girls were left. Along with Aunt Livia and Matthew, they checked out the damage from the party. The party had lasted less than an hour, but there was a *huge* mess to clean up.

"Well, let's get to work," Aunt Livia said grimly. She looked around the room and sighed.

"Aunt Livia, I'm really sorry," Amanda said for the tenth time. "We had no idea so many people were going to show up."

Suddenly, Aunt Livia chuckled. "Did your mom ever tell you about the time we had a party after a big football game, and the entire football team showed up—and the entire opposing team? The football players ended up having a big fight in the front yard, and Poppy had to break it up!"

The Chef Girls cracked up.

"So, you see, I've had a bit of experience with wild parties. With all seven of us working, we should get this place cleaned up in no time. And then we'll hit that pizza—because we'll deserve it after we clean up this mess!"

chapter 13

The next week at school, it quickly became obvious that no one thought Amanda was a huge geek. In fact, she seemed more popular than ever.

"Hey, Amanda! Molly! Great party!" called out a girl that the twins had never seen before.

"Thanks!" Amanda replied. She turned to Molly and raised her eyebrows.

In homeroom, Erica Mackenzie came over to the twins and sat on the edge of Amanda's desk. "I'm so sorry I missed your party!" she said. "I heard it was *wild*!"

Amanda smiled. "Yeah, it got pretty crazy."

"I heard that the food was incredible and that you guys are practically gourmet chefs. And that this cop came and kicked everyone out! Steve Parker said she was really tough!"

The twins suppressed giggles as they tried to picture Aunt Livia as a tough cop.

"Anyway, *wow*, I will definitely be at the next one!" Erica said.

As the bell rang, Amanda settled into her seat with a contented smile. *The party—and the party rumors!—are just what I need to win the popularity vote!*

135

Thursday morning, the twins got to school early to hand out cookies before homeroom. The night before, they had baked for hours with Aunt Livia until they had over two hundred chocolate chip cookies. Then they used pastry bags and chocolate icing to write "Vote 4 Amanda" on each one.

"I don't think I'll ever want another cookie," joked Molly. "Amanda, this is so exciting! In half an hour, everyone will be voting!"

"I know," Amanda replied. "But waiting to find out the results is gonna be a killer!"

Soon, there was a swarm of kids around the table, each grabbing one of the large cookies. "Free cookies! Vote for Amanda!" Molly yelled out above the chatter of the crowd. Within minutes, all of the cookies were gone.

The twins began to wipe up the crumbs that had spilled on the table. Homeroom was about to begin, and the hallway was suddenly quiet.

"Well, that's it," Amanda said. "No more campaigning."

"No more," echoed Molly. "Let's go vote!"

In homeroom, Ms. Lopez passed out the ballots. Amanda felt a chill when she saw her name listed.

Student Council Elections—Seventh Grade

President
- ❏ Omar Kazdan
- ❏ Angie Martinez
- ❏ Amanda Moore

Vice President
- ❏ Julia Brown
- ❏ Iris Perry

Secretary
- ❏ Mark O'Brien
- ❏ Susie Yang

Treasurer
- ❏ Tessa Allen
- ❏ Owen Michaels

Amanda made a large check mark next to her name with her favorite aqua-blue pen.

That's it, Amanda thought. *The voting is over. I just hope I can hold out until tomorrow!*

Since the election results wouldn't be announced until Friday afternoon, right before the end of school, it was hard for Amanda to concentrate in class. Still, she felt confident. *Things really came together at the end of the campaign,* she thought. *With the party and the cookies and all...*

After school, Amanda saw Mr. Degregorio carry a large box into his classroom and close the door behind him. She grabbed Molly's arm. "I bet he's counting the votes right now!" she said excitedly. "Oh, I wish we could wait around to find out *today*!"

"He wouldn't tell you, anyway," Molly said practically.

"I know," Amanda sighed. "But it's just so hard to wait."

Finally, it was Friday afternoon, ten minutes before the end of the school day. The election results would be announced any minute.

Oh, I wish Molly was here, Amanda thought as she sat in math class, curling and uncurling her toes.

Suddenly, the principal's voice crackled over the intercom. "Good afternoon, boys and girls," Mrs. Wagner said. "I have the results of yesterday's student council elections. For the eighth-grade class: Evan Anderson, president..."

Yay, Evan! Amanda thought briefly. *Oh, I hope I won. Oh, please say my name!*

"For the seventh-grade class," Mrs. Wagner continued. Amanda held her breath.

Oh, please.

"Omar Kazdan, president..."

Amanda sat frozen, stunned.

Omar won. Omar won.

And I lost.

Somehow, Amanda sat through the last moments of

class. She tried to keep a smile on her face, tried to look like she was okay with everything. But the forced smile made her cheeks hurt, and she was afraid if she blinked, tears would slip down her face.

When the bell rang, Amanda popped out of her seat and went straight for the door. Molly was already there, waiting for her. With one look at her twin's sympathetic face, Amanda knew she would cry.

"Come on, Manda. Let's get your stuff and go home," Molly said quietly, taking charge. Amanda nodded. All she wanted was to get out of there.

Amanda was silent for the entire walk home. Molly didn't say anything, either. She knew that her twin needed to be quiet. When they got home, Amanda ran upstairs.

"She didn't win," Aunt Livia said, coming up behind Molly. It was more of a statement than a question.

Molly shook her head. "Omar won," she said simply as she hung up her coat.

Aunt Livia sighed. "Poor Manda. Let's get up there and try to make her feel better." She hurried upstairs and knocked softly on the door. "Sweetness? Can Molly and I come in?" She opened the door.

Amanda was curled up on her bed. Molly could tell right away that she was crying.

"Oh, now, don't cry," Aunt Livia comforted her, sitting next to Amanda and stroking her hair.

"I'm so embarrassed!" Amanda moaned. "I can't

believe—I mean, I just really thought I was gonna win. I felt so *good* about it. And I really, really wanted to be president. What did I do wrong?"

"Don't be embarrassed, Manda," Molly said. "You did a great job! These things—sometimes they just end up like this."

"Molly's absolutely right," Aunt Livia said encouragingly. "You ran a great campaign. You took a risk and put yourself out there. You should feel so proud of yourself right now! I'm certainly proud of you, and I know your mom and dad will be when they get back tomorrow."

"But everyone's going to think I'm a loser. Why didn't people vote for me? Why did they choose *Omar* over me?"

"Hey, at least Angie didn't win," Molly spoke up.

"I know exactly what happened," said Aunt Livia. "You and Angie split the girl vote, and Omar got the entire boy vote. I have no doubt."

"Really?" Amanda asked, sitting up and wiping her eyes.

Aunt Livia nodded, handing Amanda a tissue. "Sure. Happens all the time in middle school elections. Now, cheer up, because we're going to have a sleepover tonight, and you don't want to cry through that!"

"We're having a sleepover?" Amanda and Molly asked at the same time, which brought a smile to Amanda's face.

"Yup. An emergency sleepover. Starts in about thirty minutes, so we'd better get everything together."

Aunt Livia led Amanda and Molly downstairs, where

Matthew was sitting, looking worried. "Amanda, I think you should have won!" he said earnestly. "I would have voted for you."

Amanda smiled at her goofy little brother and reached out to tousle his hair. This time, he actually let her. "Thanks, buddy," she said.

In the kitchen, Aunt Livia was on the phone with Shawn. "Shawn, Aunt Livia here," she said briskly. "We need you to come over right away for a sleepover party. Bring two funny movies. See you in thirty minutes."

Next, she called Peichi. "Peichi, it's Aunt Livia. Emergency sleepover in half an hour. Bring your favorite dance CDs. See you soon."

Amanda giggled through her tears. *Aunt Livia is nuts!*

Within an hour, all of the Chef Girls were there with funny movies, upbeat CDs, and yummy snacks. Amanda looked around at her best friends, her twin, her favorite aunt...it was hard not to cheer up with them around!

Not long after dinner, the doorbell rang.

"Now, who is that?" Aunt Livia asked, pretending to be annoyed. "I hope you girls didn't send out an e-mail about this sleepover!" she said with a wink.

"I'll see who it is," Amanda volunteered. When she opened the front door, her eyes grew wide.

It was Evan!

"Hey, Amanda," he said. "Do you have a minute?"

"Hi," she said, trying not to sound *too* surprised to see him. "Evan, congratulations! That's so great that you'll be president again this year."

"Oh, thanks," Evan said. He cleared his throat. "Um, look, I'm sorry you didn't win. You would have been a super class president. But don't feel bad about it, okay? I ran for class president in sixth grade, and I lost."

"You did?" Amanda asked.

Evan nodded. "Yeah. But I ran again the next year and won, so no big. You can always run for eighth-grade class president."

Amanda smiled at Evan. "Maybe I will," she said.

Just then, a window on the second floor opened, and Matthew leaned out. "Evan and Amanda, sittin' in a tree. K-I-S-S-I-N-G! First comes love, then c—*argh*!"

"Matthew! Shut up! Don't be a pain!" Molly hissed from upstairs as she dragged Matthew away from the window.

I'm glad it's dark and Evan can't see how much I'm blushing, Amanda thought. *I'm gonna get Matthew for that one!*

Evan grinned. "Well, anyway, I better go," he said. "Have a good weekend, Amanda. See you Monday, okay? Maybe we could eat lunch together sometime."

"That would be great. Thanks for coming by, Evan," Amanda replied, feeling giddy. "See you!"

142

"**Y**ou're back! Finally! Yay!" squealed the twins when Mom and Dad walked in the door from the airport. "We missed you so much!"

"We missed you, too, sweetie!" For a few minutes, everyone just hugged and kissed and talked at once.

"What have you kids been up to?" Dad asked, his blue eyes twinkling behind his glasses. "Almost every time we called, we got the answering machine."

"Molly and I were really busy with the election," Amanda explained. "Um, I didn't win. But it's okay. I'm not as upset about it as I was yesterday."

"That's really grown-up, sweetie," Mom said, giving Amanda an extra-big hug.

"And my pesto business didn't really work out," Molly admitted. "I think it's just *too* much for one twelve-year-old, you know?"

Dad nodded. "And how about you, sport?" he asked Matthew.

"I made milkshakes for everyone! And I tried to help out a lot!" Matthew exclaimed. "Like after the big crazy party I helped clean up and stuff. And I didn't tease the twins. Well, maybe only a little bit. Just when Manda's date came over."

Mrs. Moore raised her eyebrows. "Big crazy party? *Date?*" she asked. She looked at Aunt Livia. "What's been going on around here?"

Molly and Amanda looked at each other. *Uh-oh, here it comes!*

Aunt Livia laughed. "Oh, Barb, it wasn't so bad," she said lightly. She explained how the twins' little party had gotten out of control, and how she'd sent everyone home. "And Amanda had a date with a nice boy named Evan. He's very polite."

"You girls aren't allowed to *date!*" exclaimed Mom. "You know that." She turned to her sister. "Honestly, Livia, I can't believe—"

"No, Mom, it was me," Amanda spoke up. "I didn't think going on a date would be a big deal. I thought it would be the same as when we hang out with the guys in a group. But I didn't really like it! I felt all awkward, and I missed having my friends around."

"Well, that's good, because you two are *not* allowed to date until high school," Mom said firmly.

"No—college," added Dad, trying to lighten the mood.

Aunt Livia threw back her head and laughed. "I seem to remember a certain eighth-grader who was crazy about one Troy Gagnon, who was a *freshman* in high school," she teased Mom. "I think she even snuck out to go to a party with him once."

"Who's Troy Gagnon?" asked the twins at the same time.

"Yeah, who is he?" echoed Dad. He poked Mom in the ribs.

Mom blushed, but started to smile, too. "No one," she mumbled. Then she looked at Amanda and grinned. "I don't mind if you and Evan hang out in groups, honey. But no dating. And I want to hear all about him later."

"So do I," said Dad, pretending to look stern.

"Did you bring me anything?" Matthew interrupted, pawing at Mom's suitcase.

Just then, the phone rang. Aunt Livia answered it as Mom and Dad carried their suitcases upstairs, with the kids following right behind them.

"Amanda, it's a call for Dish," Aunt Livia called up the stairs.

"I've got this one," Molly said, grabbing the phone. "This is Molly Moore of Dish. How can I help you? Three dinners starting next Sunday? That shouldn't be a problem. Let me check with my business partners and I'll call you back tomorrow, okay? What's your phone number? Great. Thanks for calling Dish." Molly hung up the phone and turned around to see Amanda looking at her.

"You're back?" Amanda asked as a smile spread across her face.

Molly nodded. "If it's okay with everybody."

"Are you kidding? *Of course* it's okay!" Amanda squealed, giving her twin a hug. "But what about your pesto business?"

"I'm going to hold off on that one for a while," Molly replied. "There are other ways I can help people who are hungry—like volunteering at a food bank or donating some of my Dish profits."

"Your business could be part of our restaurant some day!" Amanda said excitedly. "We can call it Amanda and Molly's Place, and we could donate leftover food to charity."

"Perfect!" Molly laughed. "But maybe we should call it *Molly* and Amanda's Place."

"Well, I *am* four minutes older," Amanda said. "So my name should really go first."

Molly smiled slyly. "Race you to the top of the stairs!"

"Molls!" shrieked Amanda. "No fair!" And she took off after her sister, the two giggling all the way.

dish

The Amazing Cookbook

By

The CHEF Girls

AMANDA!

Molly!

Peichi ☺

shawn!

Natasha!

Chicken Teriyaki

1/2 cup teriyaki sauce
2 teaspoons soy sauce
1/2 teaspoon fresh grated ginger
2 pounds chicken breasts
1 teaspoon vegetable oil

1. Mix the teriyaki sauce, soy sauce, and ginger in a bowl. This is the marinade!

2. Place the chicken breasts in a casserole dish and pour the marinade over it. Refrigerate for thirty minutes.

3. Heat the oil in a large skillet over medium heat. Place the chicken in the skillet. THROW AWAY THE MARINADE— don't re-use it or eat it. Sauté the chicken for five minutes. Then turn the chicken over and sauté the other side for another five minutes.

Chicken teriyaki is super-easy—
and super-delicious, too!
I love it! My whole family does
and I bet you will, too.

—Peichi

4. When both sides of the chicken breasts are browned and the inside is cooked, remove from heat.

5. Serve over rice with some steamed vegetables on the side.

Now, wasn't that easy? And yummy!

DESSERT PIZZAS

THESE ARE SO, SO GOOD. SOOOOOO GOOD. I BET YOU WILL LIKE THEM AS MUCH AS I DO! THEY'RE GREAT SLEEPOVER FOOD.

FOR THE CRUST:

1 STICK BUTTER

1/2 CUP WHITE SUGAR

1 CUP GRAHAM CRACKER CRUMBS

1. PREHEAT THE OVEN TO 350 DEGREES.
2. MELT THE BUTTER IN THE MICROWAVE.
3. MIX THE SUGAR AND GRAHAM CRACKER CRUMBS INTO THE MELTED BUTTER WITH A FORK UNTIL COMBINED.
4. PRESS THE MIXTURE INTO A 1/2 INCH THICK CIRCLE ON A PIZZA PAN.
5. BAKE FOR FIVE MINUTES.

TOPPINGS

YOU CAN GO NUTS AND PUT ANYTHING YOU LIKE ON YOUR DESSERT PIZZA! HERE ARE OUR FAVORITE TOPPINGS:

CHOCOLATE OR VANILLA FROSTING

CANDY—ANY KIND OF CANDY!

CHOCOLATE CHIPS

MINATURE MARSHMALLOWS

CRUSHED NUTS

ICE CREAM

WHIPPED CREAM

CHOCOLATE SAUCE

STRAWBERRY SAUCE

TO ASSEMBLE THE PIZZA:

1. AFTER THE GRAHAM CRACKER CRUST HAS COOLED, SMEAR A
   THIN LAYER OF FROSTING ON TOP OF IT.

2. SPRINKLE THE CANDY AND NUTS ON TOP OF THE FROSTING.

3. DRIZZLE THE CHOCOLATE OR STRAWBERRY
   SAUCE OVER THE TOPPINGS.

4. ADD A SCOOP OF ICE CREAM AND
   SOME WHIPPED CREAM.

NOW YOU CAN EAT IT UP! IT'S SUPER-DELISH!

—AMANDA

cooking tips
from the chef Girls!

The Chef Girls are looking out for you!
Here are some things you should
know if you want to cook.
(Remember to ask your parents
if you can use knives and the stove!)

1   Tie back long hair so that it won't
    get into the food or in the way as
    you work.

2   Don't wear loose-fitting clothing
    that could drag in the food or
    on the stove burners.

3   Never cook in bare feet or open-toed
    shoes. Something sharp or hot could
    drop on your feet.

4   Always wash your hands before you
    handle food.

5   Read through the recipe before you start. Gather
    your ingredients together and measure them
    before you begin.

6   Turn pot handles in so
    that they won't get
    knocked off the stove.

7   Use wooden spoons to stir hot liquids.
    Metal spoons can become very hot.

8   When cutting or peeling food,
    cut away from your hands.

9   Cut food on a cutting board,
    not the countertop.

10 Hand someone a knife with the
    knifepoint pointing to the floor.

11 Clean up as you go. It's safer and neater.

12 Always use a dry pot holder to
    remove something hot from the
    oven. You could get burned with a
    wet one, since wet ones retain heat.

13 Make sure that any spills on the floor are cleaned
    up right away, so that you don't slip and fall.

14 Don't put knives in clean-up water. You could reach into the water and cut yourself.

15 Use a wire rack to cool hot baking dishes to avoid scorch marks on the countertop.

An Important Message from the Chef Girls!

Some foods can carry bacteria, such as salmonella, that can make you sick.
To avoid salmonella, always cook poultry, ground beef, and eggs thoroughly before eating.
Don't eat or drink foods containing raw eggs.
And wash hands, kitchen work surfaces, and utensils with soap and water immediately after they have been in contact with raw meat or poultry.

mooretimes2: Molly and Amanda

qtpie490: Shawn

happyface: Peichi

BrooklynNatasha: Natasha

JustMac: Justin

Wuzzup: What's up?

Mwa: smooching sound

G2G: Got To Go

deets: details

b-b: Bye-Bye

brb: be right back

<3: hearts

L8R: Later, as in "See ya later!"

LOL: Laughing Out Loud

GMTA: Great Minds Think Alike

j/k: Just kidding

B/C: because

W8: Wait

W8 4 me @: Wait for me at

thanx: thanks

BK: Big kiss

MAY: Mad about you

RUF2T?: Are you free to talk?

TTUL: Type to you later

E-ya: will e-mail you

LMK: Let me know

GR8: Great

WFM: Works for me

2: to, too, two

C: see

u: you

2morrow: tomorrow

VH: virtual hug

BFFL: Best Friends For Life

:-@ shock

:-P sticking out tongue

%-) confused

:-o surprised

;-) winking or teasing